TRANSITIONS

TRANSITIONS

Dave Gannaway

DeVorss Publications

11/96

11/96

© 1995 Dave Gannaway

ISBN: 0-87516-680-6

Library of Congress Card Catalog No.: 95-68720

Printed in the United States of America

DEVORSS & COMPANY, *Publisher*
BOX 550   MARINA DEL REY, CA 90294-0550

Contents

TRANSITIONS

THE AWAKENING

There was a jolt as the ambulance came to a halt. Almost at once the rear doors were wrenched open and the waiting hospital staff quickly took charge from the ambulance crew. The stretcher bearing the patient was quickly manipulated onto the waiting trolley.

Davy was aware only of the bustle of activity, his body being lurched from side to side as it sped through the corridors towards the already alerted operating room. His vision completely blurred, he was aware only of movement and color as he drifted in and out of consciousness. The jabbering voices of attendants came and went. The intermittent silence was calm and welcoming, like sleep persistent in taking over however much you resisted. His eyes rolled inward, and again the beautiful silence came. It quickly became too much to resist.

The roughness suddenly slid into calm, and in the lovely silence he became aware that he could see the group of hospital staff desperately rushing the trolley into the emergency room. It all seemed so strange. Davy could not believe his eyes as he surveyed the inside of the emergency room. He became aware that he was viewing the proceedings. He could clearly see the almost frantic activity. As he watched, remote, looking down, beyond even the gantry of lights under which the drama was taking place, the faceless green-gowned doctors hunched over a figure that could only be . . . himself.

Then he noticed the silence again, beautiful silence—and such peace. "With all that activity there must be some sounds," he thought; "someone speaking, the clink of instruments, even the rustle of their clean robes!" But the silence was deafening. He felt like a swimmer in a glass tank, weightless within the water, looking out over a world removed, a world he seemed no longer any part of.

*   *   *

There was no pain now. Quite the opposite. There was an air of elation, of wonderful freedom. Of peace. He was floating free of his body. As he looked, there was nothing visible that could be supporting his body. *Body? What* body? That *was* his body down there, the focus of all that hullabaloo. So how could he see . . . He was suddenly distracted, taken aback. Davy noticed that he was not alone. His company was a character somehow familiar.

"Oh hello," said Davy, surprised to find he was not alone in this strange place. The only response he received was a look of compassion and love. His new-found companion wiped a tear from his eye with the back of his hand.

"What's the matter?" said Davy, feeling he ought to say something. "Don't you like it here?"

His new companion looked surprised. *Oh yes; it's wonderful!*

2

"Then why can I see a tear?"

He shrugged his shoulders a little despondently. *Well, here we are again, and* still *we've done nothing. Will we never learn?* he said in quiet despair.

"Have a bit of patience! After all, it's only our first day here!" Davy was trying to console him.

Oh, you don't understand!

"Understand what?"

We didn't do any *of the things we went into the material world to do. Such a waste!*

Davy looked in total bewilderment.

Now we've got to do it all again . . . Will we ever *learn?*

"Are you saying we all had things to do when we were down . . . ?" Davy paused as he watched his companion's agreeing nod.

Yes, of course! he replied.

"Do you mean . . . we have things to do—and if we don't complete them . . . we've got to keep going back until we do?" He shifted awkwardly. "Sort of like school—if you don't get through end-of-term exams, you've got to keep going back until you do?"

3

Yes, of course! How else could it be?

"Hadn't thought about it, to be truthful," Davy replied, becoming awkward and beginning to think. "So, if we don't finish what we were there to do, before we die, then we've got to keep going back until we do!" he repeated with astonishment.

Of course! his companion said despondently. *And I so wanted to move on.*

Davy tried to console his new friend again but the tears persisted to swell in his eyes. "Oh, don't be so hard on yourself," he said. "It'll be okay . . . you'll see. What's your name?" he said, in trying to change the subject.

Fred, he replied with a sniff. *Fred Jones.*

"Jones! Hey, that's my name too! That's a coincidence!" said Davy trying to be cheerful.

Fred's glistening eyes widened, then danced in a beaming smile. *You really don't know, do you?*

"Know *what?*" puzzled Davy. He kept looking at the somehow familiar figure.

That we are the same person, you and I!

"We are *what?*" Davy said with shock.

Yes! We are the same person! I'm your other half, if you will—the subconscious part of your spiritual self. It's always been like that, said Fred with pride and delight. *If only you had listened!*

"But I don't understand," Davy exclaimed.

I know; that has been the cause of most of the trouble. You truly did not *understand!*

"But I didn't *have* a spiritual self!"

Oh yes you did!

"No; I don't even believe in God." Davy began looking around. "Seems I could have been wrong, though!"

Let me assure you that you do *have a spiritual self. In fact, you are very much a spiritual being.*

"I *am?*" asked Davy, dazed. "What is all this stuff? I've only been here two minutes and already I'm confused!"

Don't worry; you will soon begin to understand, Fred assured him.

"But who are *you* then?"

I'm the subconscious part of you—your soul-mate, if you like, Fred smiled reassuringly. *That is my job, and I've always been there. You can't imagine how frustrating it is trying to give someone help and guidance when they will not listen, and do not even know you are there!*

"*What* guidance?"

To look after you and see that you received all the help and guidance you sought—everything you wanted.

"You must have the wrong guy, Fred. No one has *ever* given me any help, more's the pity!"

It has always *been there.*

"That's a laugh! I never achieved any of the things I really wanted—none at all. You must have your wires crossed!"

Oh, I've always been there—right at your side. I can't be anywhere else.

"Oh come on! if your job was to guide and look after me and see that I received everything I wanted, what happened to you?"

Nothing happened to 'me,' Master.

"Why do you call me *Master?*"

Because you are *the Master—Master of your own life.*

"There was so much I desperately wanted to do and to have

in my life," Davy reflected; "and yet I was dogged with nothing but rotten luck."

There is no such thing as luck, Master.

"I'd like to take you up on that one, Fred!"

We will deal with it at some length a little later, Master.

"I suffered just about every indignity there is to suffer in that area, so was just a little good fortune too much to ask for?"

Indeed not; but that is exactly the point; you did not ask! said Fred.

"What do you mean, '*ask*'? You must have known! If you are always there, you must have seen that I was struggling and hurting with everything I did!"

Yes, I saw it all very clearly, Master; and I was hurt for you. But I can only do what you instruct *me to do.*

"How can I *instruct* you? I didn't even know you existed until a moment ago, so how could I instruct you to do anything?"

You never stop instructing and telling me the things you want. Every moment of every day is filled with your instructions to me—and you received every one of them that complied with our laws.

"How could I have asked for things when I didn't even know

you *existed?* I've never even *seen* you before in my whole
life!'' said Davy.

*Every time you looked into the mirror I smiled and tried to
show you how to love yourself, but you could not bear to look
with anything but contempt. I was always talking to you, but
you would never hear.*

* * *

Davy's eyes glazed over in disbelief at what was happening.

You still don't understand, do you? said Fred.

''No,'' he replied with honesty.

I am . . . he searched for the words . . . *that part of your
spiritual unity that makes things happen. I process your
thoughts into things, help you to achieve your goals.*

''Goals? *What* goals?''

Whatever it is you want from your life.

''I've never wanted any 'goals,' just the simple things of life.
I'm not a greedy person.''

You have had all the things you wanted.

''How do *you* know what I want?''

By what you think, of course. How else is there?

"Are you telling me that whatever I thought about in my physical life you gave me?"

That is a slight oversimplification—but yes. Fred continued: *What you think about most of the time is what is provided, if you are thinking in the correct way.*

"What's the 'correct way'?"

We will talk about that in a moment.

"Why was it such a miserable life, then?"

Because you were thinking miserable thoughts *is the straight answer!*

"If I were *thinking* miserable thoughts, then I must have *been* miserable!"

Of course you were miserable—because that is what you were thinking.

"Just because I was *thinking* it doesn't mean I *wanted* it."

When you go into a restaurant for a meal, you focus on what you are going to eat, not how hungry you have been! said Fred. *If you only tell the waitress how hungry you are, how can she know what to order for you? This is one of the most important lessons of all and the very reason for your suffering.*

9

"What—thinking miserable thoughts?"

Yes! But more importantly, the understanding that what you think about *sets the pattern of your life. It provides the instruction for what is demonstrated and made manifest in your life. If you spend your life thinking thoughts of lack and limitation, of failure or strife, then that is what you are asking for.*

"I can't believe this!" said Davy, lifting his arms in despair. "Are you honestly expecting me to believe this stuff?"

There can only be one truth. Let me see . . . Fred thought for a moment. *Ah yes, let me give you an example of some of your thinking, just to help remind you. Remember when you went to ask the new bank manager for a loan to finance that special business idea we gave you?*

"*You* gave me? How do you know about that, anyway?"

I *helped to give it to you.*

"Oh no. I got a 'gut feeling' about that! I remember it clearly!"

Yes, that was the one.

"Wow! that was a long time ago!"

Did no one ever tell you that you had a perfect memory?

"No . . . well, they did—but I didn't believe them!"

I can tell you exactly what you were thinking while waiting to be shown into that bank manager's office.

"Okay, then: what was I thinking?"

Fred closed his eyes as the recall spun back to him. Then in a monotone voice that resembled a talking computer, he began relating the details. *'I wish the bozo would hurry up! . . . I'm sure he doesn't like me anyway, so it will all be a waste of time . . . Look at that jerk, how could he wear his hair like that? . . . I never get any help when I need it . . . If my Daddy were rich, I bet it would be a different story! . . . Wow, what a pretty secretary! Some guys get all the luck! . . .'*

"All right, all right! I remember," Davy cut in.

So you see, you got exactly what you wanted!

"No, you've got it all wrong. That's *not* what I wanted."

That is exactly what you asked for, Master, to the letter.

"It's not what I *meant* . . ."

But it is what you said, *exactly. I've never failed you once, Master.*

"From *your* point of view, maybe; but I still had a miserable and very unhappy and limited life."

Only because that is what you asked for.

"I didn't know that *thinking* about something was talking to *you*. How could I know that you even existed?"

Ignorance of the truth doesn't make it cease to exist. If you had just been quiet long enough, you would have heard me talking to you. I was talking to you all the time.

"I never heard you, even once—honest!"

You must understand that I do not have a physical body. That is your department, so I have no mouth or voice with which to talk to you, or the use of any of the functions of a material body. I am part of the real you, an entity, a spirit. We express ourselves in a very different way. Even the rules in this world are very different from the rules in the material world.

"If you've not got a mouth or voice, you've got to be dumb, right?"

Fred smiled knowingly. *In the sense that I do not express myself verbally, yes. However, the verbal language of the physical world is so very slow and cumbersome, to say nothing about its restrictions.*

"Just how do you make yourself understood?"

By planting the thoughts or communications directly into your mind. By directly transferring ideas and information. I've heard you call it your 'gut feelings' or intuitions.

"Do you mean it was *you* that gave me all that good stuff?"

No, it was your higher self, the source of your being that works through you. It made you very happy, I remember.

"Yes; so why didn't you give me much more?"

As I said, you would not keep quiet long enough to build on our rapport, or give me a chance to demonstrate to you.

"I'm beginning to feel really bad about all this now. All those missed opportunities . . . and it would have been fun just to have known that you were there. I'd heard egghead types talking about all that mind stuff, but I thought they were, well, just missing a few marbles! . . . So you are a sort of ghost, is that right?"

No, indeed not. We are the real, *the spiritual part of you. We are as real as your arms and legs, but we are not material. You couldn't see us . . . from the material world.* Fred nodded towards the hive of emergency-room activity. *We are inseparable. Now that you have left the material body, we are united again; but while you are experiencing another lifetime we are the three parts of the single whole that is you.*

"Yeah, I get it . . . I think."

13

DAWNING

Let me tell you how it works—how the whole scheme of things functions. It may surprise you, said Fred animatedly.

"Yeah, I wish you would."

Well, as you now know, you have a conscious and a subconscious mind. The conscious does the thinking, and the subconscious—that's me—does the 'doing.'

"Yeah, I understand that. The conscious mind is what I use in the material world to think—like driving, gardening, and counting."

Yes, that's it. The Subconscious Mind is the processing part, the manifester, me. I take care of most of the important things in your life. I truly organize and run, automatically, almost everything you do.

"How can it be automatic?"

Well, answer me this: Do you regulate your heartbeats personally? Do you need to remember to tell your heart when and how fast to beat?

"Of course not."

So, if it is always being regulated, and you are not doing the regulating, how does it happen? When you use a lot of energy, run, climb stairs, or lift things, your body needs more blood pumped to your muscles. Who do you think organizes that, if you don't do it?

"The subconscious, I guess." Davy felt a little bewildered.

Yes, me; I do it for you, automatically.

"Thanks, Fred!"

And who regulates how often you need to breathe, to blink your eyes, feel tired, tell you when to feel hungry, and a thousand and one other things? That's right: I *do it,* automatically, *without your having to do a single thing. It is I, your subconscious, who am looking after you.*

"Then if you do everything for me, how come you didn't give me lots of money?"

Because you did not ask for lots of money!

"How could I ask when I never even knew you existed?"

Do you think, then, that if you are not aware of the secrets of the Universe, they do not exist? Lack of understanding is no excuse.

"Of course not; but I don't understand how I can ask for things when there is no one there to ask."

There is so much you must learn, Davy! You receive everything you ask for—if you ask correctly.

"How can you say that, Fred? My whole life has been one long struggle to survive! I can't believe that you have such wonderful abilities, yet you could have watched me suffer so!"

I have so often cried with frustration for your situation, Davy. What you must understand is, I do not have the power to change what you are thinking. That is your Higher Self, your Source—nothing to do with me. God made us and gave us the conscious ability to choose. I can produce any imaginable thing in your life—Fred held up his hands to prevent an interruption—*but only as you conceive it. It is all controlled by you. You are the master. I can do only what you ask for.*

"I never *asked* to be penniless . . ."

Yes you did, Davy. That is exactly *what you instructed!*

"No! you must have your wires crossed!" Davy snapped "How could any sane person who was having a hard time, and always struggling to find enough money just to live, *ask* for more hardship?"

Listen carefully, Davy: You decide completely *and* exactly *what I can produce in your life for you.* Again Fred raised a hand to stop another protest. *The instructions I get to work on—what I set out to manifest in your life—are exactly what you tell me you want. The only communication I, your subconscious, receive is what you* think. *What you are thinking is what I am producing in your life. I can do nothing else. I must remain totally dispassionate.*

"No!"

What you are thinking in your mind is precisely the direction that your life is heading. It's as simple as that.

"But . . . I was sick of being so short of money all the time!"

Stop right there! Listen to what you just asked for. You just said, 'I'm sick of being short of money all the time.'

"That's right, Fred. I am!" Davy was close to tears.

Davy, you have asked *to be 'sick' and 'short of money all the time'—you have just said it, can you not see?*

"What's all this about being sick?"

Isn't that what you just said and thought?

"Oh, come on! that means . . ." Davy was thinking desperately ". . . I'm fed up with having no money."

There you go again: 'no money.' It may not be what you intended, but that is what you asked for.

"No. I didn't *ask* for it!"

It is not what you meant, *but it* is *what you are asking for in your life, Master. I can only produce for you exactly what you are thinking about. Please, please, learn that lesson!*

"Fred, you're being silly. You're not in the real world, man! . . . Sorry . . . well . . . you know what I mean. Everyone understands what I said . . . Say, 'I'm fed up with having no money,' and everyone would understand exactly what it meant."

Yes, of course they would—but only those who are like you and living in lack would agree with what you said. Those who are in a better situation financially would not word it in that way. Do you think it's a coincidence that the 20 percent who have the majority of the wealth think prosperously *and do something about it, while the 80 percent who are in lack think as* you *have been thinking?*

"It's easy to talk like that, but when your situation is desperate and everyone is knocking on the door for money, it's a bit different!"

It's impossible to buck the truth, Davy.

"Oh, come on! You're not going to tell me that millions and

millions of people are having a tough time because they are using the wrong words!''

They are thinking thoughts of lack *and* limitation, *so that is exactly what they are getting. If your thinking is focused on a life of hardship and struggle, that is exactly what expands in your life. If you wake up each morning ready to face the toils and drudgery of the day, then your day will be filled with toil and drudgery because that is what you are expecting, it's what you've ordered. Haven't you ever noticed that when you get up and everything in the world seems great, the whole day goes with a swing? Everything just flows and falls into place just right.*

''Yes that's true, come to think of it; but how can you get up feeling great when you know the whole world is out there waiting to get you?''

That is a product of your own thinking. You create exactly what you want to think about. You cannot blame anyone else for that.

''Naaa, I think you're putting me on, Fred.''

If someone says something unkind or hurtful to you, it will make you feel bad, right?

''Sure.''

Then you are a victim of that person.

"A what? Oh, come on!"

If you feel bad as the result of what another person says, then you have allowed them to take over control of your mind. That allows them to decide what you think. Fred was trying not to preach yet get his point across. *God gave every human being the gift of free will, the ability to choose. If you give that gift away, then you give control of your life to another. It is your mind that controls your thoughts, and your thoughts that create your reality. What you think about most of the time is what expands in your life and becomes your reality. So your life is under the control of anyone and everyone you come into contact with. Can you see that?*

"I don't think I can," puzzled Davey.

You must understand: what you think about are the precise instructions for what you want, and I go to work to bring these thoughts into your life. If it is a life of happiness and harmony you want, why are you asking for the opposite? What do you think a waitress taking your order would say if you said, 'I don't want fish today, I am just sick of fish'? She would say, 'I don't care what you don't want, Sir, I'm just waiting to know what you do want.'

"Oh, I don't know, Fred. All this stuff is so new . . ."

Davy, this 'new stuff,' as you call it, is as old as time itself.

"Well, it's new to *me*."

I agree, and there are millions of others who still are totally unaware that there is a continuum to their life after their material existence is complete.

"I was like that until . . . now."

Indeed you were.

"But if you knew . . . why couldn't you tell us all about this stuff sooner, so that we could use it in our life? Instead of so much struggling."

Because that is the purpose of life—to learn and develop. And the only way to really learn is to discover for yourself.

"But you could have saved me so much hardship!" reflected Davy.

No. It is essential to your growth that you fully understand.

"Oh, come on, Fred!"

When you were a child, how did you learn and respect fire— learn that it could cause great pain and damage—? Yes, of course you were told by your mother what a fire would do; but before you really learned the lesson, you had to touch it for yourself and burn your fingers.

"Yeah, that's absolutely true," Davy conceded.

So the hurt, although painful, was essential for you to learn that lesson.

"I guess it was. We never listen, do we?"

It is when you do start to listen and you do start to believe and understand that you are more than just a material body, that life will become more meaningful. Once you can accept that everything which happens in your life, like burning your fingers, happens for a reason . . .

"To teach us a lesson," Davy interrupted.

Then, once the lesson has been learned that you burn your fingers when you touch a fire, you are free of it and able to move on.

"What if you touch the fire again?"

Then you hadn't learned the lesson. You see, everything is a lesson; and until you can accept that and learn, these things will continue to keep cropping up in your life. You will continue to burn your fingers.

"Is that what happened to me, Fred?" Davy asked. "Is that why everything in my life was such a struggle?"

Fred smiled and led Davy yet further towards the warm and comforting world of understanding that lies ahead.

THE PROCESS

"Would you show me how?" began Davy.

Of course. It's a simple process, if you would just do it. said Fred.

"It's a bit late now," said Davy, looking down towards the frantic activity that was continuing on his earthly body below; "but explain it to me anyway."

It is never too late, Davy.

"There can't be much chance for improvement if I'm already dead!"

Did you want to die? said Fred.

"What sort of daft question is *that*?" Davy asked.

Just a straightforward question.

"Of course I didn't want to die!" Davy thought for a moment. "I may have thought about it once or twice . . . but only because I was so miserable with everything going wrong."

But you did *think it! . . . Those were your thoughts!*

"Oh Fred, you're not telling me . . . !"

I'm not telling you anything, Davy, except that you are the Master of your own life. You have the power of free will, the power to decide your future. Fred paused, turning his attention away to the left. *Look over there . . . have a close look.* Fred was directing his attention toward a large stack of boxes and gleaming new objects.

"Whew! *That's* the car—an '87 Escort Turbo! *That* was my dearest wish back then . . . and that's the perfect color—metallic red and with wire wheels. Oh yeah, and *that's* an Apple Mac 486 computer in that box . . . and just look at all those software packages! What I wouldn't have given for that . . . and all those clothes!"

They are all yours Davy—every one of them, said Fred softly.

"They're *what?*" puzzled Davy.

They are all yours . . . they are everything you ever prayed for. Look closely and you'll recognize them all.

Davy's mouth fell open as he recognized all the objects that he had ever wanted, all piled high one on the other. All new, gleaming, and untouched.

"But Fred, *why? . . .*"

*You had the desire for them, and often you asked so
beautifully . . .*

"So why didn't I have them?" A tear formed in Davy's eye
as he surveyed all that he had ever wanted set out before him.

*Because you stopped asking before I could manifest them for
you. Sometimes you asked for things—and then you canceled
the order!* Fred smiled as he watched Davy's mouth fall open.
*So often you just would not shut up long enough to allow me
to demonstrate anything for you. Lord knows I tried hard
enough!*

"You couldn't have tried so hard after all! But how was *I* to
know? Those things would have made such a difference to my
life!" said Davy, close to tears.

*Of course they would! And as you can see, they were all on
their way.*

"So what happened, then? How could you be so cruel? You
must have known how much I was hurting."

*Of course I could see your plight, but I can only do what I
can do—and that is* nothing *until it is first conceived by you,
until you perceive what you want. If you are thinking lack,
that is what I have to create; I have no choice. You stopped
your own flow of good,* Fred explained.

"But how?"

Well, Fred thought for a moment. *Let me see . . . remember when you wanted the car?*

"How could I ever forget? I tried every possible way to get that car!"

No, not every way, corrected Fred.

"*Every* way!" insisted Davy. "I even changed banks in an effort to raise the cash. Bank managers—they've no soul, I swear it!"

It has nothing to do with that, dear friend. All that is required is to accept *it and it will be yours. So often it was all within your grasp when suddenly you canceled it.*

"How, when I was so desperate, could I possibly 'cancel' what I so desperately wanted?"

When the bank turned your loan request down, remember what you said? Fred smiled.

"You're going to tell me anyway, right?"

When the bank manager declined your request, you said, 'Oh stuff it; I don't want the rotten car anyway! What I've never had I can never miss!' Remember?

"Oh Fred . . . but I didn't mean it like that."

But that is what you said; it was what you were thinking.

"Oh no, you're talking in riddles again, Fred." Davy said in despair.

Listen carefully, Davy: what you think about most of the time expands in your life. Does that make sense to you?

"Yeah, I can take that one, Fred."

Okay. Now if you ask for money by saying, 'I don't suppose you would give me some cash would you?' what do you think would be the response? Of course the answer will be No, Fred continued. I also recall your saying to yourself, 'I really wish I could have that car.' Remember?

"So, what's wrong with that?"

What you think expands, right? Your wish to have that car is the thought that expands. Can you see that? Fred paused. So what expanded and demonstrated in your life was the wish to have that car, not the car itself. You asked for the frustration.

"Okay, smarty-pants; how *should* I think about getting a car?"

It's very simple: by accepting it—in the now: 'I love to drive my beautiful new car,' gestured Fred.

"Sure, I would love to drive my 'beautiful new car,' but I've got to get a 'beautiful new car' before I can drive it! You're not making sense, Fred."

No, corrected Fred firmly; *you have got things the wrong way around, Davy. You must* see *it and believe it in your mind before it will come into your life.* He took a deep breath and continued. *OK; let me explain the process from the beginning.*

"Right. I'll clear my mind and begin with a clean slate!"

Fine. First question: do you believe in God? asked Fred.

"No," replied Davy. "Well . . . I'd like to . . . but if there were a God, he wouldn't have let me suffer so. I've done nothing wrong."

Do you accept me *as your Subconscious Mind—the processor, if you like, that makes things happen in your life—?*

Davy hesitated. "Well . . . I guess so—at least I can see you."

So if you believe in me, then where do you think I get my abilities from? asked Fred.

"I don't know."

There is a Divine Creator of all things, Davy, a Source from which all things emanate. You and I are a part of that— whether we like it or not.

"Well, . . ." Davy hesitated. "I can handle there being a Creator or Source, but I'm not sure about God!"

That's fine. Let's stay with the Creator and Source, if that makes you feel more comfortable, said Fred.

"Okay."

Now, the first part of the process, or treatment as we sometimes call it, is to acknowledge *that fact.*

"*What* fact?"

That there is one Creator and Source of all things.

"Oh yeah, right . . . you mean like, *say* it?" asked Davy.

Yes. Acknowledge and affirm and know the truth that there is one Creator who is the Source of all things.

"Like God?"

Yes, said Fred.

"But I don't believe in God, I already told you!" said Davy.

That does not mean that God doesn't exist. Fred smiled. *You didn't believe that you had a spiritual body—until now.* He looked down towards the frantic activity continuing below. *But now that you can* see, *you can accept.*

29

"True . . . seeing is believing."

For you *maybe; but even when you didn't believe in a spirit world, it still existed,* insisted Fred. *I have always been here whether you believed it or not.*

"I still feel more comfortable with 'Creator,' " said Davy.

Then that is fine. Now let's move on to the second step, which is to accept that you are a part of the Creator.

"How can I be part of the Creator?" Davy laughed.

Everyone is part of the Creative Source of the Universe—the ultimate power that lives through everyone. That is your experience. You see, the Creator is the Source of all things . . . All things are possible to you if you will allow the Source into your life to flow through you. Fred watched as more questions were brewing.

"How do I do that?"

By accepting that it is so—that you are a manifestation of the Creative Source.

"Okay, so the first part is to acknowledge that there is one Creative Source of all things."

Acknowledge and know. *Well done, Davy; that is exactly right!* enthused Fred.

"And the second part is to understand that *I* am a part of that One Creative force."

Right—that you are a manifestation of the Source . . . that it works through you, through your Subconscious Mind.

"And that's *you*, Fred."

Indeed it is, Davy!

"Got it . . . I think!" Davy paused and looked at Fred. "So then, what's the next step, Fred?"

To acknowledge what we want to manifest in our life.

"Just a minute! How, for cryin' out loud, can we . . . "

Stop quickly, Davy! Listen to what you just said!

"Okay, okay, sorry! Let me start again. How . . . " Davy searched for an expression that would not get him pulled up. "How can we acknowledge something if we haven't got it yet?"

We just talked about that, remember? What you think about expands.

"Oh yeah; got it!" Davy confirmed.

You acknowledge what you want to experience in your life in the present tense, in the now, *as though it were already manifested in your life. As though you already had it.*

Davey's head was to one side, which meant that he was doing some serious thinking. "What if I just wanted to be alive and successful—how do I think about that, if I'm already dead?"

Two of the golden rules to remember, Davy, are not to define how *and* not to question the possibilities—*only to* state what you want. *Keep your thoughts off the things you don't want and focused on the things you do. And remember, think about them as though you were* already *enjoying them in your life, now!*

"Gotcha. So how would I say that, Fred?"

Fred looked at Davy with love and understanding. *Let me see . . .* he began. *'I enjoy my material life to the full. I am blessed with perfect health and vitality.'*

"Hey, Fred, that's brilliant!" Davy interrupted.

'My awareness of the magnificent ways of the Universe provides me with the manifestation of my every desire.'

"You've sure got a way with words, Fred! That was just great! Now, is that it?" Davy was excited.

No, not quite. There are two more steps to go.

"Even *this* is complicated!" joked Davy. "Lay it on me, Fred; what's next?"

Thanksgiving.

"What, like the harvest festival?" Davy's excitement was getting the better of him.

You normally say 'thank you' when you have received something, don't you? asked Fred.

"Oh sure. Silly me! Where's my manners? Just a cotton-pickin' minute . . ." Davy was in thinking mode again. "How can I say thank you for something if I haven't got it yet?"

Because we think as though we already have it, remember?

"Oh . . . yeah," said Davy with a vacant expression.

To give thanks and show your gratitude is a very important part of the process. You must never forget to do that, Davy.

"No, I don't . . . well, not often."

Fred smiled. *And finally, we must release the whole treatment.*

"What does that mean, '*release* it'?"

Let it go, explained Fred.

"Oh yeah." Davy thought for a moment. "How d'you do that, Fred?"

How would you *think you let go of something?*

"I dunno . . ." Davy's head fell to one side, into the thinking mode again. "Just . . . let it go, I guess," he said with a shrug.

That's right. Let it go and turn it over to the Law, the Subconscious Mind—to me, smiled Fred.

"Sort of pass the buck," Davy interrupted.

Just freeing it to Spirit. Letting it go so that I, your Subconscious Mind, can get on with my work of bringing it into manifestation. I can do nothing if you will not let it go. Remember when you tried riding a bike with two people holding the handle-bars?

"Yeah, it's impossible. I fell off!" Davy said with authority.

Exactly. So let go and free it to a Higher Power to deal with.

"Is that it now, Fred?"

I think that is plenty enough for you to absorb for the moment, don't you, Davy?

"Hey, Fred—I'm not really 'thick,' you know. It's just an impression I give sometimes."

Indeed it is, Davy, indeed it is! You're perfect just exactly as you are.

"How's that, Fred?"

That's another story, Davy. They laughed together. *That's another story.*

JUDGMENT

One of the biggest inhibitors of personal development, equal only to negative thinking, is judgment.

* * *

"Why is it that all of life's little joys are bad for us?" asked Davy.

I don't know . . . To which joys do you refer, Davy? replied Fred.

"Can't smoke . . . can't booze . . . can't talk negatively, and now the new one: can't make judgments. There'll be nothing left soon!" complained Davy.

Oh, I am sure you will manage.

"One of life's last little luxuries, gone!—giving someone a good verbal trashing behind their back." Davy laughed.

Have you ever stopped to wonder why judgment is such a popular pastime? asked Fred.

"No, to be honest."

Does it make you feel good?

"Mmmm . . . no!" Davy was not responding very positively to the prospect of another lesson.

When you make judgments about other people, you are really judging your own self. What you have to say about anyone else bears no relation to that person.

"What does *that* mean?"

Exactly that: if you judge someone to be a fool or a 'bozo,' as you say, it doesn't affect that person in any way whatever. Your saying he is a 'bozo' doesn't make him one. That's only your view. It is more you making a reflection of yourself than it is of him.

"Well, that's revealing, isn't it! Because I call some guy a bozo, you say that is what I think of myself!"

What we notice in others and criticize them about is often something that we need to deal with in ourselves. It could be made more productive if we would just recognize it as a mirror-image of ourselves. It doesn't mean that you are a bozo; but if you looked for the reason why you made the judgment or called him that, you'd discover the point to take notice of in yourself.

"So what causes me to say it?" questioned Davy.

*It's largely a conditioned habit . . . often from long ago, as
many habits are. Oh, you don't need to analyze the details
and deep-seated motives behind your judgments. Just stop
judging! Then after a while you will find that your own
thinking will change. You will begin to feel more sympathetic
and loving towards people.*

"That sounds a bit more like it."

*Yes, it is; it's a major step to take towards getting into harmony
and flow. That alone will change your whole life. Making
actual changes is the only part that takes any real effort.*

"How d'you do that?"

*Just by breaking the damaging habit of judging people. There
is nothing magic about it. If you began eating something that
was bad, what would be the first thing you would do?*

"Stop!"

*Exactly. So when you next catch yourself beginning to make a
judgment about someone, stop it that very instant and feel very
good about yourself because you did.*

"So there's no easy way?"

That is *easy, Davy. You do not need a miracle cure to do that.
Just stop.*

"OK, Fred; you're the boss!"

You know better than that . . . Master.

"It seems ages since you called me 'Master.' "

I didn't think I had to any more; I thought that was a lesson well learned!

"Yeah, it is . . . it was just a slip . . ."

Of course!

They both laughed.

FORGIVENESS

Davy was in a reflective mood, pondering many incidents that had colored his life and made him the person he had become. "In my life," he began, "I just got it all wrong." He shrugged his shoulders. "Some people make it, some don't . . . I guess that's just how life is!"

No, Davy. That is not true, said Fred softly.

"I suppose you're saying that anyone can be a success?"

Yes, of course. Everyone is potentially successful. Everyone also makes mistakes . . .

"Whew! Is that an understatement or what? I sure was successful at making mistakes, if that makes sense!" interrupted Davy.

Mistakes happen to everyone, in every area of endeavor. Making mistakes is inevitable during the process of development—any development. It is an essential part of the route to success.

"If that's the case, I should be a wealthy captain of industry!" laughed Davy.

Let me explain the reality of errors. Just recall steering your car—say, driving along a perfectly straight street. You are constantly turning the wheel to the left and right just to keep the car going in a straight line.

"Yep, I got that," Davy nodded confidently.

As you steer from one side to the other, the car momentarily moves off in the wrong direction. Then you compensate by moving the wheel back in the opposite direction. You are oversteering—making 'mistakes' and then quickly compensating for them. You learn to do it instinctively, without thinking. Each movement begets an error that is quickly corrected. Although the road may be straight, the track of the car is not. Yet all the while, the car is moving forward ever closer to the goal. So if you were to condemn yourself for every error, the car would quickly run off the road and not reach the destination at all. It's the same with all of life's errors. Fred paused for a moment.

"So what should I do?"

Forgive yourself and let it go. It's a part of the development process, a step closer to your goal.

"That's pretty clever in theory; but where did I go wrong?" Davy puzzled.

If your life is out of sync and nothing seems to go right, it's a fair indication that you need to do some work on forgiveness.

"Well that's me, Fred!" said Davy confidently.

Fred smiled knowingly without speaking.

"You knew that, didn't you? Hey, you've been peeping at my life again!" Davy joked.

Indeed, Davy; I do truly know you better than you know yourself.

"Yeah; that bothers me sometimes. A chap needs a little privacy now and then . . ." He felt a little uncomfortable for a moment.

Not from himself, Davy.

"Okay, you win. So I need to do some work on forgiveness," Davy said, changing his focus.

It would make a great difference. You see, there are three areas in life that create the need to forgive.

"Only three?" joked Davy. "I think I could fill a book!"

There are just three areas: blame, revenge, and judgment. Once they are brought to heel, your life will be unrecognizable from how it is now.

"I like the sound of that, Fred."

42

While these areas fester unchecked, your natural and spiritual progress is slowed or even stopped altogether.

"It makes that much difference, eh?"

Yes. Once we can release those three areas, the lights of your progress will all turn green and the way will be clear to move forward.

"That's important!" Davy agreed.

Yes, said Fred looking directly into Davy's eyes. *You already do it for others.*

"I *do?* . . . So I can't be *all* bad!"

There you go already, making judgments.

"But I was only joking, Fred."

Don't make jokes like that, Davy! Remember, what you say is what expands in your life!

"Correct. So tell me more about what I've been doing that's right."

I recall, quite often, times when various folks took you into their confidence and told you their troubles, said Fred.

"That's quite true; but I don't see what that has to do with forgiveness." Davy's brow wrinkled.

Can you recall your response to those people?

"No, not really," Davy said honestly.

Once they had told you all their troubles, you responded in the same way every time. You were so reassuring. You would say, 'Oh, is that all? Don't let it bother you—everything will turn out fine. Just forget it; let it go.' Remember?

"D'you mean I did something *right* for a change?" asked Davy with surprise.

Indeed you did. You showed and encouraged forgiveness and compassion, thus allowing them to free themselves from their hurts. This is the important point for you: you know exactly what to do for others; *but when it comes to* you, *you give yourself a hard time.*

"I don't understand what you are saying," said Davy, puzzled.

I am simply saying that you have the wonderful quality of forgiving everyone else yet you beat up on yourself when things go wrong in your life.

Davy thought for a moment, knowing that what Fred was saying was true. "Yeah, I make me sick, don't I?"

Yet it is that very forgiveness that frees us from our past hurts, freeing us to live our lives in the now—*to stretch and grow.*

"Surely I'm not to blame for *everything?*"

Blame is so often the bogey that runs out of control. When things go wrong, it is too easy to lay the blame at the door of someone else instead of taking responsibility ourselves.

"Responsibility . . . for *everything?*"

Yes; because who you are, at this very moment, is the result of what you chose to accept and believe. You have taken it on board.

"But what if someone upsets me or makes me mad?" Davy raised his shoulders.

They cannot make *you upset, or angry, or anything you do not choose. If you feel angry or hurt, then it's because you chose to feel like that,* said Fred.

Davy's head was to one side—its "thinking" mode.

The only person who has access to your controls is you, continued Fred. *When you can accept* that, *you will have learned an important lesson. I am not saying that the hurt or hatred is not real. Of course it is; but it is real in your experience because you gave it permission to be. You allowed someone else to have control of your mind.* Fred paused a moment. *The irony is that whoever gave you the hurt in the first place is probably totally unaware that anything ever happened.*

"He got off scot-free!"

He has always *been free, just as* you *are free. It is not he who is to blame because you took his insult. He didn't* dispense *it; you took it—without his even knowing!*

"So what is the answer?"

To forgive and forget!—just as you correctly tell everyone else: 'Don't let it worry you. Let it go.'

"So I'm not really doing it all totally wrong?"

Of course not. You are wonderful just the way you are! Understand that and stop beating up on yourself. You already have many wonderful qualities that make you a very special person.

"I have? . . . I mean, *I have!*"

Indeed you have, Davy. Forgiveness is essential if you are to grow spiritually. Once you can forgive, your light shines yet brighter. Not to forgive can only strangle your growth.

"Whew! You really make things sound so good, Fred."

Everyone has the power to forgive, Fred spoke slowly. *To forgive effectively, you must begin with yourself.*

"How's that?"

You must stop being so hard on yourself. Forgive, forgive, forgive! There is nothing useful or of benefit gained by brooding over mistakes.

"But how?"

Just know that you have the sublime power to overcome any adversity once you can forgive yourself.

"So that's the project, eh? . . . to forgive myself," said Davy.

There is no other way if you wish to grow spiritually. Fred paused for a moment. *If you think you should be punished for the wrongs or mistakes you have made, then you certainly will be, because you will punish yourself. Likewise, if you know that the Universe is all-forgiving, you can escape—indeed reverse—the effects of anything. Forgiveness is the very essence of Love.*

Fred's words embraced Davy. He continued:

Learning to forgive is also an important part of learning to love yourself. Remember, there are no accidents, Davy. Those events and people that are unwelcome in your life are your opportunities to learn the lessons we all need. So when you have learned the lessons sent to teach us to forgive, they will no longer be necessary.

"Are you saying that once I can forgive and let go, then all the stuff that caused so many problems will stop?" Davy asked in surprise.

Yes, of course! Why else would you have them? You do not have challenges and problems out of deliberate nastiness. Everything has a reason.

"Then *how?* If I do something wrong, I must pay the price, surely?"

If that is your belief, then that is true: punished you will be, but not by the all-forgiving Creator. You are punishing yourself. So if you can forgive yourself and let it go, then that is the end of it. All judgment is within you—not the Creator. It is all right to make mistakes, Davy. Great successes can often be the result of mistakes and failures.

"How so?"

Did you know that Edison made a thousand attempts at inventing the light bulb? Fred became lighter.

"Is that a fact? Boy, he sure had staying power!"

Such was his faith, Davy. He let it go when things went wrong. He knew that each mistake, each failure, was another step closer to success.

"Yeah; I guess he was a bit special, eh, Fred?"

Yes indeed he was special; but then so are you, Davy.

"Oh, you say the *cutest* things!" Davy joked.

Only because it's true. When you say to others, 'Forget it, don't let it bug you, let it go,' that is the truth.

"Good medicine, eh, Fred?" Davy laughed, preening himself.

Yes—if you would just use it for yourself.

"Why is it, Fred, that I can give so much good advice yet don't take it for myself?"

Why do you think, Davy?

"Search me, Fred."

I'll tell you: because of your own poor self-esteem.

"I *thought* you were going to say that!"

I know you did, Davy; but you didn't mention it, because you didn't think you were smart enough to know the answer, right?

"Right on, Fred! It's really great having a friend who knows you better than you know yourself!"

Thank you, Davy; but everyone *has, if they would just accept it.*

"True, but that's just the point: *they don't know*—just as *I* didn't know . . . until I . . . met you. Oh, I often wondered if there were more to life than I knew about; but I *did not know.* Life would have been so different if I had known some of this stuff!"

These are times of change, Davy. More people than ever before are now becoming aware that there is more to life than just what looks back at them from the mirror.

"But how can they find out?"

Everyone must learn for themselves. Have you never heard the expression 'self-discovery'?

"Yeah, I've heard of it," Davy replied.

Well, that is what it means. Everyone must discover the truth for themselves.

"Why not just tell 'em?"

That just doesn't do it, Davy. What did you say when your friend tried to tell you about spiritual matters?

"I told him to get lost! . . . Oh, yeah, I get it! . . . "

Exactly! You were not ready to hear it, right? The whole process depends on self-discovery—discovering for yourself the true wonders of what lies beyond the material world and just who we are.

"That's the most exciting thing, Fred. I feel like yelling it from the rooftops. Ain't it great?"

It certainly is, Davy; it certainly is.

BRAINSTORMING FOR CHANGE

"I know I need to make some changes but I don't know what!" Davy said.

This is something that has been frustrating you since you first contemplated the subject on Monday 5th April—the day you were twelve, Fred reminded.

Davy's mouth fell open in amazement at the precise and instant recall of such specific detail. "I can't *believe* it!"

That's why you can't do *it, Davy. Let me see now; that was the day when you brought a school friend home for a snack. Ah yes! His name was Lawrence, he lived on Magnolia Drive, he was a very talented artist—but what appealed mostly to you was his refreshing flow of imagination. In particular, the balsa-wood models of space vehicles he made in such precise detail. He gave you one as a present that day—you recall it had doors and hatches that opened, revealing details of the cockpit, cargo hold, and engines.*

"Oh Fred, that's exactly right—it was beautiful! I thought so much of that model; how I envied him! I wonder what became of it?"

The model got damaged and your mother threw it out.

"Oh *no!*"

She thought you had discarded it as you had so many of your other things.

"That's a shame. Lawrence was just so talented! I'll bet he's a famous artist or a NASA scientist by now!"

He works in the administration section of the Ford Motor Company.

"No!" Davy said with disbelief.

He has worked there for thirty-four years. You've seen him many times in your home town but failed to recognize him riding his bicycle.

"Oh, that's too bad; I'm really surprised at that . . . such a waste of a beautiful gift! He probably keeps it as his recreation."

No, he has rarely made models or pursued his painting since leaving school. His hobby is aircraft-spotting, which he shares with his son.

"Well, that's amazing! I wonder why?"

He grew up.

"That's crazy. We *all* grow up."

Yes, that's true, Davy; but sadly for most people, the stereotype of growing up is that we stop playing like a child and enjoying life, and start thinking and being 'grown-up.' That, Davy, is a major paradox, because children's creativity reflects their uniqueness; and just as it is developing beautifully—Bang! they become adults and destroy it all. At once the world becomes a serious place full of unbelievably cruel realities, when only yesterday it was full of fun and child's play. Will we ever learn?

"Hey, Fred: that was negative!" delighted Davy.

Regrettably, yes; it was very remiss of me, admitted Fred.

"That's all right—just a slip of the tongue, eh? Just goes to show we're only human." Davy laughed.

No; I am not human, Davy.

"But it's all right anyway!"

Thank you. Where were we? Fred asked.

"We were talking about Lawrence."

Ah yes: he unfortunately experienced a severe cultural shock.

"A *what?*"

As his high-school days drew to a close he became influenced by the false lure of the material world—of money, to be precise.

"What's false about that?"

It is not possible to create banknotes in the same way as you produce a lovely picture, Davy. The money comes as the result of producing the pictures or items of imagination, then finding people who want to exchange money for them. It is a metamorphosis of the truth.

"Whew! I don't grab *that* one, Fred!"

It is a total transformation from one way of thinking, and of perceiving the world, to another. In his case it was, sadly, away from the truth.

"But surely you understand that he obviously needed to earn some money, just as I did, just as we all do."

Of course; but tell me, Davy: what comes to mind when you think of money?

"You gotta get out there and earn it! . . . got to work . . . get a job . . . hustle . . ."

That is the error of your thinking, Davy.

"What is?"

Seeing money associated only with those things—all things you consider and believe 'hard' and by inference unpleasant. So your dominant belief is that to have money to survive and live, you need to indulge in the distasteful, unpleasant pastime called work, which by nature is 'hard' and demanding and difficult and most often poorly paid.

"Yep, that about says it all, Fred!"

It does indeed; it just about tells the story of your life, does it not?

"You got it, baby," said Davy, relating fully to Fred's analogy.

Davy, please listen carefully: you have what is often called a working mentality . . .

"OK, I'll buy it. What exactly is that?"

It means that you relate money to work. That to earn a lot of money, you have got to work very hard and suffer the consequences. It also follows that you believe that to receive money, or anything else of value, without suffering and hard work is not worthy of you or honorable.

"Yeah, that's right. How can you have money without hard work?"

Let me show you how limiting *your thinking about this is.*

Answer me this, Davy: imagine you worked very hard digging holes in the ground for a whole week to earn three hundred dollars. Your next-door neighbor works in an office, fewer hours than you, yet he takes home four hundred dollars for his week's work.

"That's where it's all wrong!" snapped Davy.

But is it all wrong? Could it not be that you have got it wrong?

"How can shuffling papers from behind a desk, with lily-white hands that never get dirty—how can that possibly be worth more money than someone who's working hard?"

There's hard work other than manual work, Davy.

"Aaaa," Davy's face contorted with contempt.

EXPECTATION

It is very probable that if three people—let's call them *A*, *B*, and *C*—were to do the same mental work for abundance, their results would be very different. Not because there was any difference in the way they did their mental work, but in what their expectation was. If *A* was used to receiving $100 for a week's labor, *B* received $500, and *C* $1000, then even though the mental process was precisely the same and successful for all three, the amounts realized would be precisely equal to their expectations. Thus *C* would continue to manifest ten times more than *A*.

* * *

Think about this, Davy. Take your time, because I want you to see how important it is, began Fred.

"How important *what* is, Fred?"

The way your thoughts have affected your life. I have already told you several times that what you think about is what you experience in your life.

"Yeah, I can go with that."

What has been the content of your inner thinking and mental attitudes over the years corresponds precisely to what you have experienced in the material world.

Davy's eyes glazed over as he wrestled with the thought. "Yeah, that's about the size of it, Fred."

It is exactly *it, Davy. It is known as the* mental equivalent *or the* expectation level. *Your outer world of experience will precisely equal your inner thoughts and convictions.*

"But it wasn't all my fault! My thinking was no different from my mother's and father's and most of my friends'."

Exactly right, Davy. It is a conditioned response: group consciousness.

"I don't know about that!"

Don't worry. Just understand that you had faith that life was intended to be traumatic and difficult. That was your consciousness, your expectation. It was what you expected to happen, and that was precisely what you experienced. Right? asked Fred.

"Right," agreed Davy. "But it wasn't my fault—not all of it," repeated Davy.

That does not alter the facts. The Subconscious Mind is impersonal: It doesn't know any difference between plenty or lack, difficult or easy; It only does. *It is totally dispassionate.*

"What does *that* mean?"

Simply that no matter whose fault it was, if you were thinking and expecting it, that is what It produced in your life.

"That's not fair!" Davy protested to Fred's great amusement.

Fairness has nothing to do with it. That is what you were thinking, so that is what the Law of Mind produced in your experience. If you were to touch live electrical wires, what would happen?

"I'd get a blast!"

Indeed you would, Davy. So would anyone who did that, whether it were you, the President of the United States, or the smallest baby. If they touch live wires, they get a shock. It is the Law, and the Law cannot differentiate. That is why you cannot enter a prosperous reality while poverty commands your thoughts. It just cannot be done.

"The story of my life, eh? What a mess!" Davy said soulfully.

No, Davy; it's a time to rejoice! said Fred excitedly.

"Rejoice! If I weren't already dead, I'd feel like putting an end to it all!"

No! Can't you see? Now that you perceive the errors of your thinking, everything will change. You now know how to make yourself free. Life can be wonderful from now on—if you learn the lesson.

"But I'm dead!" Davy bemoaned.

Do you feel *dead?* asked Fred.

"Well . . . no, not exactly . . . But I am, aren't I?"

EVERYTHING IS PERFECT

Your life is, right now, *exactly as it should be*. This is one of the most beautiful concepts imaginable. Everything in the Universe, in the world, in ourselves, is exactly as it should be for this moment in our lives. That may at first appear a controversial statement; but if instead of entertaining controversy we open to the possibility of a new understanding developing within us, then we will experience an acceleration of awareness.

* * *

"You are saying that everything is exactly as it should be?" asked Davy.

Yes, replied Fred, adding to his surprise.

"Let's be sensible, Fred. How can everything be perfect and just as it should be?"

Before you allow it to contort your mind into a knot, let's look at it in another way.

"Okay, but make it easy!"

Instead of trying to unravel the knot, let's go back into our past and ask the same question again.

"All right; but how do we do that?"

Simply let your mind drift back to a time in your past.

"What time?"

Any time you choose—could be ten years ago, when you got married . . . at school . . . whatever you choose.

Davy's head dropped to one side as he slipped into his thinking mode. "Yep, got it,' he said after a moment's contemplation.

So you recall being a teenager of fourteen! said Fred.

"I don't know if I can get used to you being able to look into what I am thinking almost before I know myself!"

Why?

"Well, you know . . . what if the thoughts are . . . well . . . private?"

You cannot have private thoughts in the spiritual world. Only in the material world, where people are wearing the mask of a body, can you conceal thoughts—and then only *to the material world. But we are digressing again.*

"Sorry, Fred; we were going to discuss my thoughts of being a teenager."

Ah yes, he said more comfortably. Now, as your thoughts and awareness are back at the time when your earthly clock says you were fourteen years old, recall the details—let them all flood back . . . what challenges were facing you, what was bothering you. Recall some of the things you did and were in the process of doing. Let it all flood back into your awareness as if it were today.

"Whoa, that's not easy!"

You are saying that out of habit, Davy. What could be easier than remembering? Just locate that time and be there in your awareness. The rest will flood in like water into a pool, each detail supporting the other, finding its perfect level. Everything is driven and fed by the other. Pick up one strand and everything else will weave itself into the reality of that moment. Just allow it to happen. You can't force anything or make it happen—only allow it.

* * *

Davy sank into deep awareness of that time. Gently his thoughts filled the full spectrum of the particular moment when his body was fourteen years old, every detail emerging gently one by one through the mist, fitting perfectly into the order and perspective that was his life. Everything was there in a multidimensional awareness, a return to a past reality, exactly as it had been, yet strangely different—different because he was now viewing it as an adult, through an awareness that had matured and grown with the help of time's perspective, like a football player viewing the game a second time from a place high in the stadium rather than on the field of play.

He sat there in his bedroom full of all the frustrations of living in a world where people just didn't understand or maybe didn't want to. "All I want to do is build boats. What could be simpler than that? Why should I have to learn all this irrelevant nonsense?" He was half-heartedly doodling in the margin of his math homework. "What possible use could this be to building boats?" Picking up a boating book, he was quickly absorbed in the distraction, bathing in the beauty and form of the sweeping and arching timbers of a beautiful yacht. There was a magnetic attraction that outshone math to such a degree that the pleasure totally consumed the moment.

* * *

Fred's words echoed from a distance outside the fourteen-year-old's reality.

You can see why you were such a good boat-builder and so poor a student, can't you?

Davy did not reply. He remained in the young man's frame, and Fred was in "talk-over," as though he were narrator to a film. *Gently bring yourself back to the reality of now.* Fred carefully reestablished Davy's awareness back in the present moment.

"Whew, that was strange! It was like déja vu in reverse! I could feel that I had experienced it all before, yet something was different."

What do you think was different?

"I can't make it out, exactly. Everything was just as it was, yet . . ." Davy puzzled ". . . it was different!"

That's because you were looking upon it from a different viewpoint. Your perceptions of life are far more mature now than when that took place. You realize now, for instance, the real value of the math knowledge you allowed the robbers to steal from you.

"Yeah, I really should have studied that math."

No, that is impossible. You cannot 'should have' done anything. That is neurotic thinking. It is done and complete, and nothing we do can affect that.

"It doesn't get away from the fact that I should have paid more attention to math. It robbed me of so much!"

Yes, it truly did rob you of so much; but please stop that illogical 'I should have' thinking. That can only lead to negative progress and a lowering of your self-esteem. The only logical, positive, way to deal with it is to say, 'I need to work on my math now!' said Fred, watching Davy's eye's defocusing in bewilderment.

"Well . . . if you say so," he said, totally perplexed.

You cannot now *work on math for when you were fourteen, can you?*

"Don't be daft, Fred; of course not! . . . Sorry—didn't mean to be rude."

With all that 'should have' thinking, you are developing beliefs of failure. You are telling yourself that because you did not do whatever, you are now a failure!

"Yeah, that's right—I *am*," said Davy with an agreeing nod.

No, you are not! Fred raised his voice. *So stop telling yourself that you are! Remember, what you think about expands. So if you are thinking, 'I should have done this' and 'I should have done that,' you are developing pure* failure *thinking. If you want your life to develop towards your purpose for being here, you must accept that everything is just as it should be.*

"Okay, I got that now."

Nothing from the past could have been any different from how it is right now. Okay, now that we have that out of the way, we can begin to move forward—to fulfill our life's work.

"How can I be sure what that is?"

The only way is to go within and ask, said Fred with a smile.

"Meditation, right?"

Exactly.

"But couldn't you tell me what it is, Fred? I'm only asking," said Davy with a roguish smile.

Yes, I can. Your task is enlightenment—to learn how to give love unconditionally, move out of judgment, still anger and bitterness, and allow the truth of all that is to permeate your life—but most of all to forgive. Is that detailed enough? asked Fred.

Davy's jaw dropped. "Yeah, thanks . . ." He swallowed deeply at the awesomeness of what his life was about.

Making this shift in your awareness will produce the biggest and most profound changes you have ever made in yourself.

"I can fully appreciate what it will do, Fred; but I just feel out of my depth at the moment. I don't think I have ever made a 'shift' before; in fact I wouldn't know one if it came up and bit me!" Davy replied with eyebrows raised. "You say, 'all you've got to do is think differently,' but when your thoughts have been running riot as long as mine have . . ."

You are letting the robbers get their toes in the door again! All they will do is steal your ideals.

"Right now, I just couldn't give a . . ."

Oh yes you could, Fred cut him short. *But you have actually got to make the shift. It's not sufficient to* know *about it; you must* do *it—make the changes and integrate them into your life.*

"I don't know where to begin!"

Fred smiled knowingly as he watched Davy in his bewilderment. "Will it make me feel any different in myself?" Davy asked.

Very much so! Most noticeable will be your focus: it will shift away from the material. The money, cars, and collectibles will no longer be the prime desire of your life.

"Oh Fred—does that mean that I will not be able to have those . . . all those things I've . . . ?" There was a tone of disappointment in Davy's voice.

No, Fred added quickly; *quite the opposite, in fact. When you can shift your focus from wanting, wishing, and willing to* knowing, *all of those things will become manifest.*

"I don't understand that, Fred."

Then don't even try for the moment, Davy; just accept the information as a gift with the love with which it is given, and accept that you already have everything in the world you've ever wanted. You have everything in your life right now.

"I've *what?* I've already got *everything?* But . . ."

No 'buts,' Davy. When you can accept it in your awareness, those things that have been denied to you thus far will begin arriving into your life. But it will begin only when you can release them from the focus of your desires. Willing *them into your life with all your might is creating the very block that is holding them back.* Stop willing *them and start* permitting *and* allowing *them. That is what opens the door!*

A longer-than-usual silence ensued. Davy was even more bewildered than ever before. The real test of understanding, the truth about paradox was stretching him to the limit.

"Fred, I need you to run this by me again . . . slowly."

Just relax and allow your mind to visualize what I am saying: You arrive at a surprise gathering that has been arranged as a special treat for you. Everyone you ever wanted to meet, or be with, is there and feeling warm and positive towards you. There is a genuine love and caring. The air is full of joy, and you suddenly realize that everything in your life is just perfect. You are in such perfect harmony with everyone and everything, just so happy that you could burst. This is all that could possibly matter; this is the true meaning and power of life.

There is not a care in the world. You do not have to put on any airs and graces or worry about appearances or what people think. Everyone loves you just the way you are, and you love them back, perfectly happy with the world and everything in it, just the way it is.

Then as you are getting used to being in the ultimate state of flow, the awareness of pure joy, you notice that all of those material things you ever wanted are there waiting for you. You are delighted and very happy when suddenly you realize and understand that they are not the key to your happiness. It suddenly becomes as clear as crystal that the most precious thing of all is the love, the joy, and the harmony that you can now feel flowing through your very existence. Like a magic sprinkler system that operates from within, you know that this is how you intend to spend your life. This is all anyone could ever desire!

"That's real fairy-tale stuff! Sounds like you've been on dope!"

It does, doesn't it? But you don't need drugs, to get a high on true reality—that is just how it works, Davy! It's what those people on drugs are chasing.

"It doesn't make one ounce of sense . . ."

Exactly right! As you know, it is all a paradox; so you would not expect it to make sense, would you?

"Okay, it's a paradox. So all the things I want, and have been bustin' a gut to get since I was knee-high to a grasshopper, I've got to let go of and stop wanting! Right?"

Right! Easy, isn't it? Fred smiled. *Just release them into the flow.*

"Now how can anyone take that seriously, Fred?"

Very easily. It seems we should take another look at the topic of knowing *before continuing.*

KNOWING

Can you remember how, when you began working in the boat-building trade, you marveled at the ease with which the journeyman shipwrights coaxed seemingly rigid timbers around the complex and curving shapes of a hull?

"Sure I can! I always thought that it was the most fascinating thing in the world."

And can you remember when you first tried to do it for yourself? Be honest, Davy.

"Yeah; I snapped 'em every time!"

Can you remember what you used to say about it?

"Sure! I would call it a . . ."

No, not what you called it in your frustration. The comments you made.

"Yeah; I always thought it was impossible. You know I did. You can remember better than I can!"

You would grow more and more frustrated because the timbers you were working would break; yet the journeyman shipwrights would bend them around with infuriating ease, remember? Fred recalled.

"Will I ever forget! They'd bend 'em around without even trying."

Davy, say that again, said Fred. *The last thing you said!*

"What, 'They'd bend 'em around without even trying'—" Davy repeated with wonder.

Without even trying. They knew the timbers would not break . . . they had a knowing *. . . and once you developed the skill and knowing, it was the same for you.*

"Yeah, that's true; I can understand that, Fred. But letting go . . ." he puzzled.

Things only went wrong with the timbers when you were trying *not to break them. When you were totally focused, intent, and concentrating on not breaking them, what happened?*

"They broke!"

Once you knew—*once you approached them with a confident 'knowing,' an attitude that didn't even consider the possibility of failure—you enjoyed success. You did not even marvel at things when they went right, because there was no doubt in your mind that they would. So of course they did!* Fred smiled as he continued. *I remember very well when you were learning to ride a bike, how your Dad would run alongside holding on to the saddle, keeping you balanced. How good it felt! Then, when he was totally winded, he said, 'Okay Davy, I'm letting you go—you are on your own!' You screamed, 'No, no!' . . . and crashed into a heap.*

"Yeah . . . and hurt myself!"

Then, when your Dad was again running alongside keeping your balance, he let go of the saddle—but still ran alongside.

"He *did?* I didn't know that!"

That's right, you didn't know *that he had let go, so you continued riding perfectly. It was not his hand that was balancing the bike; it was* you! *Only when your* knowing *discovered he was not holding you did you begin to wobble and fall off.*

"But it didn't take me long after that to learn," said Davy.

Of course not—because every time you fell off, your Dad sat you back on again until you learned and believed *you could do it. Once you stopped allowing the doubting robbers to steal your belief that you could do it, you very quickly developed a knowing.*

"I know without question that everything you are teaching me is correct, Fred; but how do you go from total doubt and *not knowing* to *knowing?*" Davy puzzled again.

75

By knowing *from the very beginning! Now that you are aware of* knowing *and of the robbers that want to steal it from you, you just don't allow them in. Remember, think only about the things you want, not what you do* not *want. By just not thinking about failure and things you don't want to happen, you are taking charge of your own life. Once you stopped thinking about the timbers breaking, they stopped breaking. When you stopped thinking about falling off your bike, guess what? You stopped falling off!*

"Hey, that's really beginning to make sense now! The mist really seems to be clearing!"

That's good, Davy, that's really good! Maybe now we should return to purpose!

UNITY

The concept of Unity, or oneness, is difficult for a purely material person to perceive. Just as most other universal realities appear as contradictions, Unity is no exception. Yet the concept is integral to a meaningful understanding.

We may see ourselves as individuals, separate and independent from each other, each doing what we need to do in order to make our lives function. Is that how it really is? Or is there more to life than that?

* * *

We are all one, all part of the One Great Creator of all things, said Fred, making himself comfortable.

"I've never really been able to take that on board. How can we all be one? It sounds as if we're all Siamese Twins, all stuck together like a great big bucket of worms!"

That description doesn't quite cut it, Davy.

"I didn't expect it to—but neither does the idea of us all being one!"

Just imagine for a moment that you were sitting in the shade of an old barn. It has a rusty old tin roof, and up there in the tin is a little hole . . .

"Yeah, you'd see a little beam of sunlight shining through, right?"

Right. Now imagine that the beam of light is an umbilical cord that connects you to the sun. He held up a finger to stop another interruption. *Now, if the sun were your Higher Intelligence, the Source of your being, and if It radiated Its love and all-knowing communications to you along your own personal beam of light, you would be personally connected with that One Creative Intelligence. Would you agree with that?*

"Sure . . . Hey, that's neat! Yeah, I can understand that."

But wait a moment, Davy; there's more to this example than that. You see, everyone has their own personal beam of light, their own little hole in the rusty tin roof, that connects them to their Higher Source.

"Of course. The sun shines on everyone. Yeah, I got it."

Good; because to understand that we are all as one, and yet individuals, is a wonderful and very important step forward.

"It is? You mean that we have all got a connection to the Higher Consciousness?"

Exactly. And because, like the sun, It is universal, every single one of us is connected to It and to each other. We are all one—but even more than that, you see, Davy, you are a creation of that Source. Without you at the end of that sunbeam, It would have nothing through which to create. You see, the Creator works through *you. You are Its means of manifestation—Its hands and legs, if you will.*

"So how come God needs *us* to do things through? Why doesn't He create things directly Himself?" Davy asked.

Because you are an expression of God. Without you and everyone else, nothing could be manifested into the world of form. That is the wonderfully Divine nature of things. It's the ultimate expression of Love.

"Hey, hold on a second! What about those who speak a foreign language? How will *they* understand?"

There is a universal language that does not require the use of words. When you are in Love, that Love radiates out and expresses itself in many ways other than words.

"Yeah; I never thought about it like that before. That's really clever."

Yes, you *are,* Fred replied.

"No, not me; I meant *you* are really clever, Fred. I'm just a dummy, remember?"

I know what you said, Davy. So if you are a dummy, as you

say, then you think I am a dummy also, and your Higher Self and God too?

"Heck no! I didn't mean to be rude. I only meant . . ."

I know what you meant, Davy, but it is what you say and do that is important, because what you say is a reflection of what you are thinking.

"Okay, I got it. I didn't mean to be rude. I'm sorry." Davy spread his arms in surrender.

Fine. Fred collected his thoughts again and continued. *So if we are all one, then* you *must be clever also, right?* Fred noticed a wavering of Davy's attention. *You* do *see that point, don't you, Davy? Think about it. It is very important to clearly understand. It will make a big difference once you do.*

"You mean that because I'm connected to the sun—I mean to a Higher Consciousness—then I am also connected to everyone else, even people on the other side of the world who can't even understand my language?"

Exactly. Well done, Davy; that's great! Fred could see the progress.

Just as the beam of the sun's light connects you *directly to the Higher Intelligence, so the beam itself also illuminates everything else with its light, so that we can see many things that were hidden from us before. That is the medium by which*

*everything is, quite literally, all connected. That makes us all
one. Let's look at it another way: imagine yourself as an
electric light bulb instead of a person, and everyone is a light
bulb—although not every bulb is lighted or turned on. But
your light is on; you have allowed the flow of power into your
life; you are connected with the source.*

"You're into the power lines, right?"

Yes, but more than that Davy, Fred continued with feeling.
*. . . more than that. Being connected with the Source lights
your bulb and it is* your *light that radiates out to illuminate so
many wonderful things that, until that time, were hidden from
you. Things that were always there but eluding you because
they were hidden in the darkness.* He paused for a moment.

"Who ever notices the beauty of a light bulb that's *out?*
Right, Fred?" asked Davy. Fred's reply was the beaming
smile of a teacher whose pupil had just graduated.

That's it! You've got it, Davy!

After a few quiet moments, Davy's head dropped to one side,
signaling that his mind was in its "thinking" mode and was
incubating a question.

"But it doesn't *always* work, does it, Fred?"

Oh yes, it *does; it's the* people *that often prevent it from
working, the* people *who cut off their supply. This is exactly*

*what I meant when you first came over, remember? I said,
'Will we ever learn? Will we ever find ourselves on this path?'*

"What path?"

*The path of knowing . . . the switch that lights the bulb
. . . the hole in the tin roof. That is the path that leads to
understanding, to the truth of what is. Or, as you would say,
'where it's at'!*

"Hey, right on, Fred! You're all right!"

Once on the path to enlightenment, progress is exciting . . .

"Does it take forever, and lots and lots of lives, before we
'get' all this stuff?"

*Everyone is an individual, Davy; they progress at their own
pace. Total enlightenment and oneness is in every soul's
destiny; but how long it takes is not important. Being on the
path is what matters.*

"So you can take as much time as you like?"

There is no such thing as time, Davy.

"There's not?"

*How long, in earth time, would you think we have been
talking?*

"Oh, must be weeks." Davy instinctively looked at his watch.

Davy, look over there: can you see? Fred guided Davy's view to the frantic activity taking place in the emergency room, where surgeons raced to "save" his life.

Davy looked incredulously. "That only just happened . . . I had an accident and . . . but we've been talking for . . ." His jaw fell with the unfolding of his first lesson in this new reality.

* * *

There is no such thing as time in the nonphysical world. It is something that we have invented for our convenience, to help with our calibration and understanding. In the world of thought, Fred and Davy's conversation could have lasted fifteen minutes or fifteen days. Both would have been the same. They could have talked about one small topic or lived a whole life, both in the same period, just as in our dreams we are able to cover centuries with the same ease as we cover a fleeting moment. In one moment you can be a child, the next an elderly person. There is no time between.

Davy intuitively knew and felt this to be so, yet his material perception, or reasoning, had difficulty in dealing with it. For it transcends the boundaries of language or material logic, and so becomes a paradox.

LESSONS

Davy made himself more comfortable as his interest in Fred's conversation grew. "So what sort of things will it work for?"

Anything you can believe yourself to have.

"What about a Rolls-Royce?"

Can you see and believe yourself owning a Rolls-Royce at this time in your life?

"No; 'cause I'm dead!" Davy rocked back with laughter.

Don't be so sure; those surgeons working on your body down there may win their battle and save your earthly life.

"Hey, no! I don't want to go back there, Fred! It's great here!"

However, we didn't do what we were sent to do. You may have to go back!

"Then you'd better give me all this stuff quick, in case I need to leave in a hurry!" Davy laughed again, though not so happy at the prospects.

So answer the question: could you see *and* believe *yourself owning a Rolls-Royce?*

Davy put his head to one side and thought for a moment. "No, not really."

Then that is the answer to your question.

"But if I can only see myself with an old jalopy . . . that's not a lot of good, see? I've already got one of those!"

Well, that's very good, smiled Fred.

"It is?"

Because right away we've identified one of the limitations that are holding back your progress. You have been asking *for an old relic, and that is exactly what you have* got. *Ain't it great?* said Fred with a wry smile.

"I don't get it," said Davy.

In your mind, you saw yourself with an old relic of a car. Isn't that right?

"Yeah . . . but that didn't mean that I wanted . . ."

That is what you were asking *for. That* was *your experience at that time,* Fred interrupted excitedly.

Davy shook his head desperately. "If you need to be able to

picture the things you want in your head, and I can't do it, then I'm out of the running, right? And that's probably why I didn't have those things before!'' His eyes turned down despondently.

Fred smiled and said warmly, *That is exactly right, Davy, exactly right. But isn't that exciting?*

''*Exciting?* No, it's not! Nothing's simple!'' he barked back.

Everything is simple—but it is sometimes not easy. *Remember, Davy?* Fred's loving smile took on a wily look. He knew exactly how irritated his student was becoming.

''Oh, that's just another play on words! 'Easy,' 'Simple'— *what's the difference?* It doesn't change the fact. *I can't do it!*'' He was beginning to wave his arms around.

Ah, but you can *do it, Davy! Don't you see? Each of the little challenges that crop up in our lives is a lesson we need to learn, an area where we need to know a little more.*

''The way we're going, *the whole of my life* is going to be one long lesson! Never-ending!'' Davy fairly snapped.

Yes! Fred leapt up with delight. *That's exactly it! You're getting it, Davy, you* are *getting it!* There were tears of happiness in his eyes.

''So what's so great about that, eh, Fred? It's okay if all this learning stuff turns *you* on; but . . .''

Fred stopped his flow. *Davy, stop right there and listen.* He stilled the air with his hands, then continued slowly. *That is life. That is it—the whole pattern of things. Remember, when we first met, we talked about how we had things to do in our earthly lives; and if we didn't do them, we just had to keep going back, lifetime after lifetime, until we did—?*

"And we couldn't move on to another level until . . . ? Yeah, I remember."

That's it! Try to see, Davy: these are those lessons, the things you must learn before you can move on. They are the ways and the rules of the true Universe. You can't begin to function as who you really are until you have learned the lessons and know the rules. Fred paused for a moment. *It's all so simple! You can do it, can't you see?* You can do it!

"But there must be more to life than just all this learning!" Davy's protests were becoming weaker.

You are still under the negative impression of learning that you had when you were in school, rebelling against everything because you couldn't see any sense in the things you had to learn. All you wanted to do was ride your motorbike and make boats. Davy, these lessons are different!

"How?"

They are lessons about life, *about the* rules. *As you learn them, things in your life will change. You'll learn how to have things, how to change things. Most of all, you will take charge of your own life. Stop being a victim and become master of your own ship!*

"What if I don't *want* to be master of my own ship?" the rebel persisted.

But you do, Davy; you do.

"I don't know," he hesitated. "I'm not sure I can handle the responsibility."

Have you thought what the alternative is? To always be a 'worker bee,' at the beck and call of any and everyone, spending another life as a victim wandering aimlessly through another life out of control, giving up all your choices to someone else: a re-run of your last life, Davy. Remember all the pains and heartaches—all to be relived again at another time in another place . . . all for the sake of finally taking responsibility for yourself. Fred left his point running wild in Davy's mind.

"Mmmmm. No . . . if you put it like that . . ." The rebel was conceding.

You paid the price for that all right, didn't you?

"How d'you mean?"

Look at the jobs and fine positions many of your classmates from school attained in their lives!

"What is this, some sort of interrogation?"

No, Master. It is the most important lesson of all.

"Why d'you call me Master again?"

Because you must learn to become the master that you are. Captain of your own life and your own destiny.

"But I'm really not sure I can do it. Am I the sort? If anyone should know, it's you."

Of course you are. Everyone is. But before anything can happen, you learn to take total responsibility for your life. That's all!

"But I *do,* don't I?"

No, Davy. But just understanding that will begin turning your life around. An awareness of the ways of the Universe will lead you to everything you have ever wanted and more. Remember what Jesus said in the Bible: 'He that believeth in me, the works that I do shall he do also; and greater works than these shall he do.'

"You're not going to start getting religious on me, on top of everything, are you, Fred?"

No, Davy; religion has nothing to do with it, he said kindly. *Shall we return from our digression?*

VISUALIZING

Now where were we? Fred asked.

"You were teaching me how to visualize things in my mind."

Ah yes, that's right. Fred paused to realign his thoughts. *A little practice is all that's required; and very soon everything you can see with your eyes open, you will be able to see with them closed—and a great deal more.*

"*More?*" exclaimed Davy.

Oh yes; much *more! With your eyes closed, you move into the nonmaterial realm of the Subconscious Mind—another world completely; a world with none of the restraints of the physical world. There is nothing you cannot do in your mind, Davy.*

"I'm not sure . . ."

There are no limits of any kind. You can travel to the farthest corners of our globe in as long as it takes you to blink. You can swim to the bottom of the deepest ocean or fly to the nearest star, just as easily as . . . that. He clicked his fingers. *But let us return to the matter of visualization.*

"Yeah, we'd better!"

To begin with, there are many different methods of approaching this vast subject; but we will use just one for now. Sit quietly and still your mind.

"How do you do that—still your mind, I mean . . . ?" asked Davy.

As you spend a little time each day sitting quietly and practicing your visualization, it will quickly become easier. Imagine the pictures, or objects you wish to see, on the bottom of a pool of water. While the water is disturbed, the objects on the bottom of the pool will not be visible. But as you allow the water to become still and calm, what you seek will come into view.

"Whenever I've tried to clear my mind and think of nothing, it made things worse."

One of the spiritual truths you will quickly come to learn is to simply let go *and not do anything. Simply* be in the now. *It is from there that so much will happen. When the physical body is at rest, it allows our Higher Self in, so to speak; and when you can begin to communicate at that level, things begin to happen, and progress becomes more rapid.*

"So relaxation is where it's at?"

The process is commonly known as meditation.

"I don't want to become a monk and shave my head or any of that stuff!"

If you feel happier with 'relaxation' then call it that, Fred laughed.

"What's the difference?" asked Davy.

Relaxation is a process of relaxing the body to relieve physical stress. Meditation goes much further. It relaxes the mind and stills that internal jabbering. Imagine a glass of muddy water when it is allowed to become still. The sediment will settle, and the water becomes clear.

"Hey, that's really clever, Fred! Why can't I think up stuff like that?"

You will, Davy—when the water clears! He smiled.

"Yeah, right! So how do I get into meditation?"

To begin with, find somewhere comfortable where you can be undisturbed. Somewhere away from as many distractions as possible.

"That's why those guys head for the mountains, right?"

Something like that, Davy; but it will work fine right where you are. So, to begin with, just sit quietly with your eyes closed.

"Do I have to sit cross-legged on the floor?"

No, Fred smiled. *It's quite sufficient to sit comfortably in an upright chair with your feet on the floor. When you are comfortable, focus your awareness on your breathing. Then effortlessly go to your maximum level of relaxation.*

"I can do that. *Now* what?"

Then, in the peace and harmony of your quiet place, bring your focus on a single object.

"Like what?"

A beautiful rose or the flame of a candle, maybe. It can be anything.

"That's just the trouble; when I close my eyes, I forget what they look like!"

That's fine—then practice sitting quietly looking at the rose or the candle with your eyes open.

"Yeah; I can do that."

Focus on it in every detail for a few moments . . . and then gently close your eyes, taking the picture with you into your mind. Continue to see it. Fred spoke gently and paused, watching Davy.

"That's neat; it really works . . . for a moment; then it's gone again and I can't remember what it looks like!"

Fine; do it again, this time making the inner picture last a little longer. Remember, practice makes perfect. You will really discover the benefits if you discipline yourself to regular practice.

"I think I've got it, Fred. I'm on my way!" Davy was getting excited.

So where were we? Fred asked.

"You were saying how one needs to want things that are believable."

Ah yes; I remember now, said Fred slowly. *Yes, you have to believe that you can achieve whatever it is, and see it as a natural part of your life.*

"Like being rich?"

What is being rich, Davy?

"Having lots of money, of course!"

How much is lots *of money? You see,* lots *of money to a penniless vagrant may be enough money to buy himself a good meal and warm bed for the night, but to a more prosperous soul it could amount to millions. Everything is relative.*

"Yeah, I get that. So you need to be specific."

Yes indeed; but even more than that, Davy. Let me see . . . verbal languages are so limiting. He stroked his chin while he thought. *Let's say, for example, that you decided to be a baseball player.*

"Wow, that's a laugh!"

Exactly; and the very reason it would never come into being is that your belief system cannot see *it as a reality. It is beyond your reality to perceive.*

"But if I were into baseball and that was what I really wanted and could see myself doing . . ."

Yes, exactly—now you are getting the right idea. We will talk more about setting goals later, but for the moment let's focus on what we are doing.

"That's okay by me, Fred. So, we've got a clear picture in our mind of exactly what it is we want, and we truly believe we can have or do it and that it would fit in perfectly with our life."

That's right—you need to be able to visualize it as though it were a perfectly natural part of your life, right now.

"As though I've already got it!"

Yes, of course. If you were to visualize it in the future, then it would always be in the future. It would never actually arrive.

"Like 'tomorrow never comes'!"

Exactly. Good thinking, Davy! You visualize everything in the present, in the now. *See yourself being the* you *you want to be, in the life you want to lead. Be there—totally, not only visually. Experience* everything—*the feelings, the touch, the taste, and the smell. We have five senses: use them all.*

"Like get excited?"

Excited, fulfilled, secure, loved—whatever it is that is important to you. Make it so real that you are there. Then when these beautiful thoughts are fully developed and complete . . .

"What does that mean, Fred, 'fully developed'?" Davy interrupted.

Quite simply what it says, Davy. Go back to the example of baseball. If your desire were to be a great baseball player, that thought alone would not fully satisfy your desires.

"It wouldn't?"

No; because the fulfillment of such ambitions requires more than just to be a great baseball player.

"What then?"

If I helped you to become exactly what you asked to be, you would indeed be the 'best' player—but that would be all. It could be the best player on the school team, or the best player in the Little League.

"Oh come on, Fred! If a guy wants to be a great baseball player, he's gotta mean in the major leagues, be on TV, lots of money—you know the scene!" said Davy, arms outstretched.

It doesn't mean anything, because it doesn't say anything. That is the vital point to learn and understand, Davy. What you say is seldom what you mean!

"It's not?"

No. Successful thoughts must be specific: *a great baseball player, playing on a* specific *team in a major league. Visualize it clearly and happening in the* now. *See yourself walking out onto the field to the cheers of the crowd, feeling the buzz and scoring the winning run—being there in that very moment.*

"Hey, Fred, that's really great! I feel real excited just thinking about it!"

You see, it is so simple, *Davy; yet you have been making it so* difficult—*as you have already discovered.* Fred's reminder of his past life's disappointments soon dispelled Davy's exuberance.

"So is that what I was doing wrong, back then?"

Yes—one of the things.

"Hey, I thought you said this thing was simple!"

It is *simple; but I didn't say it was easy!*

"What's *that* supposed to mean?"

What could be easier than seeing in your mind exactly what it is you want and then asking someone else to get it for you?

"Ask someone else? *Who?*"

Me, of course, said Fred with a proud smile.

* * *

The very simplicity of the process produces skepticism. Seeing and experiencing the object of your desire as though it were a part of your material reality at this very moment in time is the very process of creation. Experiencing it in every one of the five senses brings the desires to the very doorstep of material reality. To identify yourself in the visualization qualifies you as the recipient; and to assume a *knowing assurance* that these delights are already a part of your material existence, as are the clothes on our back, confirms the inevitable existence of them in your life.

* * *

"All this sounds manageable so far. What's next on the list?" Davy asked.

The most important part of all. Yet it is the simplest.

* * *

There began a silence that was alive with its anticipation and that survived the temptation of either to speak, lest it break the spell. The aliveness of the moment, however, spoke volumes; and a new understanding and realization that the limits of the unspoken word could never capture cracked across a silence unencumbered by the dulling fog of logic. An age passed in a moment.

* * *

"What was *that* all about?" asked Davy, breaking the spell.

Did you feel something happen?

"Yeah . . . but I couldn't exactly describe it."

Don't try, Fred smiled. *Don't try.*

DETACHMENT

*Did you really understand how thoughts are everything,
and how they produce everything in our lives?*

"Yeah, I think so. You were telling me how what we think
about grows and expands in our lives," said Davy, making
himself comfortable.

That quite literally is true, said Fred, trying to get a handle on
what he wanted to talk about. *Everything is possible if we can
think in the right way.*

"What about miracles?" asked Davy jokingly.

Miracles most of all!

"Oh come on, Fred! You'll have me believing in fairy tales
next!" laughed Davy.

*Davy, fairy tales have a very important part to play in
developing our awareness.*

"They do? I thought fairy tales were for kids."

Yes, exactly. Our adult abilities to use our powers of

imagination and visualization are based on our childhood development. Having a vivid imagination is often, quite rightly, considered a gift—but it is based on the foundations laid in those childhood years. It is a very important part of our basic awareness. Much is to be learned from such tales, yet even they *have been corrupted to the point where they fail to fulfill their function.*

"You're missing me with this one."

It is by learning to read this type of literature that young children begin to discover the meaning of life and its possibilities. Through fairy tales they live and visualize fantastic things, open up opportunities to do anything from flying through the air to traveling to a distant star.

"If they can read, that is!"

Exactly. It is just so *important that young people learn to read and get into a reading habit.*

"Who needs to read when you can see it all on TV?"

That is the danger.

"Danger?"

Yes. Remember? You were trying to learn how to visualize.

"Yeah; I always had a problem seeing things in my mind."

That may be the result of not having learned the delights of reading when you were very young. You see, when you read—however slowly—the words from the page create pictures in your mind. This is how the imagination develops the ability to visualize. The words from the page create images within the mind—pictures created with the imagination. That is quite literally creation.

"I can understand that; but TV does all that for you!"

All TV does is show you someone else's imagination.

"I guess that's right."

And if we don't develop the ability to read and exercise these abilities, we can lose much of life's meaning. Like most things, if we do not use it, it will fall into disuse and fail to work. Ever notice when the TV is turned off how many children go into a state of near panic and complain that there's nothing left to do? Their fertile minds have stopped functioning for themselves and become dependent on TV.

"Use it or lose it—right, Fred? So what's that got to do with fairy tales?" Davy asked.

Well, it's these early childhood stories that exercise and develop the imagination—although it's very interesting that most of the traditional fairy tales as we know them today have been changed and have lost the very purpose of stimulating a child's fertile mind, mainly because of movies and TV.

"Are you saying Walt Disney's got it all wrong?"

In a way, yes. Of course he was unquestionably a creative genius and quite rightly the hero of millions. Yet it was this same genius that unraveled and explained the stories in every detail, making it unnecessary for children to use their own imagination. They have been sterilized by his amazing skills of storytelling. There is nothing left for children to visualize and imagine for themselves.

"And adults!"

Yes, of course. It has become pure entertainment.

"So you think he should be banned?"

Goodness, no! He has become an important part of our culture. All I suggest is that children be encouraged to read and to develop the wonderful gift of imagination for themselves. You see, Davy, even when a mother reads a child a story from a book, the child is creating its own movie in the mind, its own visualization of the story—and that is so very important.

"No doubt about it. You're a wise old owl, Fred!"

Traditional fairy tales have been adapted and changed to suit the large and small screens and the taste of millions of people, young and old. For example, in the traditional tale of Little Red Riding Hood, she was actually eaten by the Big Bad Wolf.

"Hey, that's a bit strong! I thought all fairy tales must have a happy ending. Shouldn't they, Fred?"

Yes, quite right, Davy, they do; and that is the very point: how Little Red Riding Hood, or Little Red Cap as the traditional story was known, overcomes and learns all the lessons the story presents—real lessons from life. Finally, after being eaten by the Big Bad Wolf, she is rescued by being cut out of the wolf's stomach.

"Hold it, Fred! That's more like a horror movie than Disney!"

Indeed it is; but the visualization and imagination provide the answers to the lessons. Thoughts of succeeding against impossible odds are precious lessons indeed, Davy.

"That's more like miracle thoughts."

Yes—and exactly what is needed! The child is saved by a miracle and lives happily ever after. What a perfect lesson! Thoughts and imagination make it all possible, just as in life— and before the inflexible material logic of cause and effect takes over and stifles the mind, encasing the imagination in a straightjacket. The child's imagination creates a world where everything is possible.

"Hey! You've got something there, Fred!"

Those are the very qualities that need to be developed in our lives. Anything is possible for every one of us, not just for great talents like Walt Disney or Steven Spielberg. Everyone can do it!

"Even me—right, Fred?"

Most of all you, Davy. You see, watching too much TV, which young people do, exposes their fertile minds to the seeds planted by the TV networks rather than to their own imaginations. And the TV networks aren't always interested in our young people's minds. They want to market products and make profits.

"To get us to buy candy and toothpaste?"

The young minds are rather at the mercy of these companies than beholden to the wonders of their own beautiful imaginations. Even more important, they are denied the experiences and benefits of the full and prosperous life that personal visualization and imagination incubate.

"D'you think that is why I achieved so little?"

That is a lesson you must learn and understand, Davy.

"My eyes were always glued to the TV, and I had great problems visualizing things, didn't I? And just like you said: if the TV was turned off, we were really down, because all our time was spent glued to it."

Fred remained silent, his face reflecting a love and understanding that gave Davy the assurance he was looking for.

"It's all a bit late now—isn't it, Fred?"

Oh no! Learn these few basic lessons, and progress becomes very rapid. Once you have chosen your route, every step takes you closer to the goal. But without understanding, any step is merely a shuffling in the dirt and remaining stationary.

"It must be great having that sort of imagination—like Disney or Spielberg, I mean," said Davy, still thinking about fairy tales.

But you have—*if you would only develop it! Did you ever hear the story of Aladdin and his wonderful lamp?*

"Sure; that was one of my favorites. I always loved the idea of having a genie that would pop up whenever he was needed."

Fred smiled knowingly. *When we talk about people like Einstein, Mozart, Disney, or Spielberg, what collective word would you use to describe them?*

"All I know is they were all geniuses."

Exactly. And where do you think the word genius *comes from? That's right:* genie. *The link has always been there.*

"That's really clever, Fred! You must have been really smart in school."

Ignoring Davy's idle chatter, Fred stayed with the meanings of various words.

There are several other words in the earthly, material language that give a hint of spiritual understanding.

"There are?"

Take the word insight. *The literal meaning would be 'a sight from within.' What about* inspire—*the dictionary definition is 'to guide or arouse by divine influence.' Another meaning of* inspire *is literally* 'inner breath.' *That's interesting isn't it?*

"You must have swallowed a dictionary—you left me on the first bend! I understand what you're saying, but this time it's me who's short of the words to describe what you taught me."

They both laughed and agreed that, for the present, any further knowledge would render Davy's mind totally ineffective.

THE GIFT OF TALENT

Many of the great talents, both past and present, credit much of their skill and achievements to a Source beyond their physical self. Those who have become liberated by these beautiful gifts often talk freely on how this wonderful, often miraculous, information arrives, their techniques of accessing it, and the profound changes it made to their lives. (The less enlightened, while still receiving guidance, are often reluctant to disclose the source of the information.)

* * *

It has long been well established that highly talented people credit their gift to their Higher Self, or the Creator, said Fred.

"D'you mean the talents of those great artists and brilliant guys have got a handle on the Higher Self and all this stuff?"

Yes, of course; there's no doubt about it.

"Well, how about that! So they're not *really* talented—it's *given* to them. They get it from 'up there.' "

Does that make them any less gifted, Davy? That is *the gift! That is where everything comes from. It is well documented how many of the great artists, composers, and writers credit their Higher Self, or higher guidance, for their creations.*

"Like who, Fred?"

Well, a classic example is Mozart, the genius composer. His letters reveal how his works came to him as a great gift from his Maker.

"Does he mean God?"

That is something you must interpret for yourself, Davy. Mozart said that most of his ideas came to him when he was relaxed and alone and that he could not force them, but that they would flow gently into his awareness, where they would 'fire my soul' to write them down.

"And that's what made him famous!"

Of course.

"Some people get all the luck! . . . oh, all right, I remember." Davy stopped himself. "There's no such thing as luck . . . Well, some people get all the *opportunities*."

It is there for everyone, if you would just understand. The great laws of the Universe do not apply to one and not another. They are totally impersonal and applicable to all alike.

"You would think so, sometimes. I wish I could get stuff like Mozart did, or even just a little to make things flow a little easier. I'm not a greedy person."

There you go again, limiting yourself, Fred said, interrupting him.

"What did I say *now?*"

You said you didn't want much success. Well, you haven't got much success, have you? So can you see how limiting that remark was? Could you imagine Mozart saying, 'I only want to write a mediocre concerto today'?

"Well, you know what I mean!"

No; you must learn and understand that what you say *is a reflection of what you are* thinking, *and that what you are* thinking *is what* expands *and* manifests *in your life.*

"I've really got to work on that, haven't I?"

Yes! Because it is so very important! You would not go to the grocery store and ask for flour if you really wanted tea, would you?

"No, that's insane."

Well, it's exactly the same, Davy. You must *change this habit of asking for the opposite of what you really want.*

110

"Okay. Now, will you tell me about Mozart?"

All right, where was I? Ah, yes. You know, Mozart wasn't the only one to receive inspiration and guidance like this. Almost all creative and talented people have experienced it in one way or another. The history books are full of examples.

"Such as?"

Robert Lewis Stevenson.

"Who's *he?*"

Have you never heard of the book Treasure Island?

"Oh, sure I have! I just loved *Treasure Island* and the guy with the peg leg—what was his name?"

Long John Silver.

"That was it! 'Ahhhh, Jim 'awkins lad . . . them as dies'll be the lucky ones!'" said Davy in his impersonation of Long John Silver. "That was a great movie! Who was it . . . ?"

Robert Louis Stevenson . . . it seems his characters are better known than their creator.

"And he got all that from his Higher Self?"

The ideas for many of his stories came via his dream helpers.

He called them his 'Brownies.' He records that the key to communicating with these inner helpers was 'not to think consciously,' but to drift into that beautiful state of reverie that lies between being asleep and being awake, and to allow it to naturally and effortlessly flow into the consciousness.

"Yeah, I know what he means—that beautiful in-between, 'dozy' state when you're not really asleep and not properly awake."

That's it. Technically that is known as a hypnopompic *state, but 'dozy' is perfectly adequate.* They both laughed, enjoying their comparisons.

The methods of accessing such inspiration vary from individual to individual. There is no right or wrong way to do it, Fred continued.

"So how do you start?"

By just asking and trying something. Edison would sit and watch the clouds float by until he drifted into the blissful state where he knew that the answers could be communicated. Another did it while riding a noisy trolley car or horse and carriage. The secret, Davy, is in opening your mind to receive. *Imagine it as a large, open sponge that is ready to absorb whatever comes its way.*

"That's good, Fred."

*You have got to want help then, as the Zen masters say:
'When the student is ready the teacher will appear.' Many
wonderful things have made their entrance into the material
world via a dream, one of the most famous being the invention
of the sewing machine.*

"Who was that—Mr. Singer?" suggested Davy.

*His name was Elias Howe. The story goes that he had
completed the invention of his 'lockstitch sewing machine,' as
he called it, with the exception of the needle. He racked his
brain and became extremely frustrated that such a small detail
should hold up his success. Then one night in a dream he was
sentenced to death by a tribe of warriors when he suddenly
noticed that the spears they carried had eye-shaped holes in
the head of their spears. That was it, that was the missing
link. He awoke in a frenzy of sweat and excitement, knowing
he had the answer he sought. The eye in the needle of his new
machine needed to be in the pointed end, the opposite to the
traditional needle.*

"Wow, that's a great story, Fred! But the dream sounded
more like a nightmare to me!"

*But isn't it amazing how a nightmare like that can affect the
whole world?*

"The whole world? That's a bit of an exaggeration!" asserted
Davy. "It can only affect the girls with their sewing machines,
right?"

*What about the factories that produce your clothes and the
millions of other items that are made from cloth and fabrics?*

"Yeah; I didn't think about that. You're right—of course!"
said Davy. "So where do these ideas come from?"

From your Higher Self. You may prefer Creator, God, *or your*
Higher Consciousness. *It is important simply to know that It
works for* you *in* your *life. It will help in anything and everything you do, and all you have to do is* ask *and then shut up
and listen. Nothing could be easier than that, surely?*

"Fred, I've said it before: you're a marvel!"

*Thank you, Davy; but all I ask is you understand that
everything I've talked about applies to* you. *Mozart,
Stevenson, and all the rest have shown us how it was for
them, and now you must let the same happen for you.*

"I don't know what to say!"

Don't say anything!

"I've never had anyone concerned about *me* before."

*Just understand that you are the most important person in
your life. You are perfect and exactly as you should be right
now. It's all right for you to be successful and prosperous; it's
not just for the other guy—it's for* you, *Davy. Love yourself
and let it flow into your Life.*

CREATING IDEAS

It always seems such a mystery to pose the question "Where do my thoughts come from—where does an idea begin its life?" Davy had learned much from Fred. And with so much having been revealed to him, so many answers, so many truths, his mind was incubating the ultimate question! Making himself comfortable, Fred was ready.

* * *

That's a good question! Fred began.

"*What's* a good question? I didn't ask a question yet!"

Oh, sorry, Davy! You wanted to verbalize it first? Okay, go ahead.

"Huh?"

Do you want to speak the question or do you just want the answer?

"What was I going to ask, then?"

Where do thoughts come from! Fred replied.

"How d'you know I was going to ask that?" wondered Davy, surprised.

That was what you were thinking, wasn't it?

"Yeah; but I didn't say anything yet! So how did you know?"

Speaking is such a cumbersome way of communicating!

"Speaking's *what?*" Davy screeched in surprise.

You don't need to speak to communicate!

"Are you telling me you've got a handle on my brain that I don't know about?"

It's simple enough to know what a person is thinking without their speaking. You do it all the time to some extent. All it requires is a little more practice. It's the same with reading; why do you beat around the bush, struggling to make out every single word on a page when you could see them all together?

"Just a moment. Slow down some, Fred. What does *that* mean?"

When you read, what do you do? You start with the first word and work your way along the lines, right?

"Fred, don't tell me you've got another way? You wouldn't

start at the last word and work your way backwards by any
chance?'' Davy asked cynically.

*No. Look at them all together, or at least large groups; it is so
much easier to understand things that way.*

''How can you do that? It's impossible.''

*Answer me this, Davy: if you were shown, in total darkness,
into a room you have never been in before and the light was
turned on for one second and then off again . . .*

''Sort of a flash?'' interrupted Davy.

*If you like. Just a one-second flash. How much of the inside of
the room do you think you would have time to see?*

''Everything, I would imagine. It only takes a flash to see
what's there, doesn't it?''

*Exactly. In that second you would just see everything,
wouldn't you?*

''Sure!''

*There wouldn't be time to see each item in the room
individually—a table here, a chair over there, the blue
carpets, two windows (one open). You would just see it all as
one—just a particular room—as a picture, if you like; just as
though you clicked a shutter and took a photograph in that
one second of time.*

"Yeah, that's just about right."

So why can't you look at the print on the page of a book and do the same?

"But that's different!"

No! It's only because you say you can't. Your association with reading is probably based on the old belief that you have to work at each and every word individually. That's the only thing that is different.

Davy was stuck for words. He knew and understood what Fred was saying, but he couldn't find the words to continue his half of the conversation.

When the author of a book gets an idea of what he is going to write about, he or she sees it as a whole, as large chunks of information to be transferred to the reader—not as individual words. On their own, the words do not say exactly what he wants to say, so he weaves them into a block, a chapter, a section that uses them to interpret exactly what he wants to convey.

"Sort of like an artist massing all sorts of shapes and colors on a canvas; it's only when you stand back to look that it resembles a picture!"

Yes, or a sequence in a movie. Just how the director weaves the individual pictures together creates the mood or interpretation he requires. The same scenes could be restructured in many different ways to convey a whole range of interpretations.

"Yeah; that's a good example," said Davy, catching up.

So, with reading, the more you can absorb chunks of text, the closer you can often get to the author's true and original line of thinking.

"How did we get to talking about that when we set out to talk about where *ideas* came from?"

All these things are linked, Davy. The inspiration and ideas that are communicated by the artist's or the writer's Higher Self are what he or she then tries to communicate to the material world through the artwork or the writing.

"Almost like he was given an extra special secret."

Yes, an extra special secret that he knows must be passed on to everyone; yet he knows that if he related the truth of how it came to him, it would sound so fantastic or far-fetched that no one would believe him.

"Yeah, that's right. If that were me, I think I'd just keep quiet about where it all came from!"

That is exactly what has been happening, Davy. Great people have not revealed the 'secret' of their greatness—where their inspiration came from. Instead, they have bathed in the glory of their success without revealing from whence it came.

"Is there anything wrong in that?"

Nothing wrong as such; but it is time to share 'the secret.' There is a great desire for news from the Other Side. Great awareness is developing, and we must share.

"What if they don't believe?"

You can feed only the hungry, Davy.

"Hey that's clever! That really gets to it!"

THE MOMENT OF CREATION

We have talked about where ideas come from. What do you imagine happens to them once they arrive in the material world? When you ask for help or information, what if you don't act on it or use it?

"You must be loony, I suppose," said Davy.

Not always—if you are not aware. Oftentimes people are not aware of the ways of the Universe and unknowingly *solicit information.*

"What d'you mean? Ask for something without knowing?"

Exactly. It happens all the time. An idea could be placed right under your nose but you might be unable to see it or perhaps to recognize it for what it is, so that nothing is done with it, and it remains unattached and drifting. It has been brought into creation and just left.

"You mean that one is too lazy to do anything with it?" Davy asked.

Could it be that once an idea is created, it comes into some sort of 'cosmic' form? Then once it has this form, it would be available to anyone who was able to tap into it. This would account for the amazing fact that many new ideas burst into life almost simultaneously at opposite ends of the earth. Have you ever had a brilliant idea come to you and, instead of doing something about it, you procrastinated and did nothing —and then, a while later, you saw that someone else had done it, had produced exactly the same thing?

"Hey, you *know* I have! That's exactly how it was with that idea I had—I mean you gave me—but I couldn't raise the money to do it. And then just a few short weeks later I noticed someone else doing exactly the same thing!"

Yes, that's common enough. Now, how do you think that happens?

"Search *me*, Fred!"

When you get an intuition—or 'gut feeling' as you say—you receive what I can only describe as an idea. *It is something that arrives in your brain from seemingly nowhere.*

"Right; I'm with you, so far!"

That moment when the idea, or inspiration, clicks into your awareness is the moment of conception—the very first moment when that idea comes into existence in the conscious world. Do you remember me talking about the hole in the tin roof and how, through that beam of light, not only you but everyone is connected to the Source, the Higher Consciousness?

"Go on, Fred; I'm keeping up."

Now this beautiful new idea arrives in your consciousness.
You have conceived it, you have given it life, if you like.
You have brought it from nothingness into the somethingness
of your conscious awareness. That, in itself, is a miracle.
However, since it has now traveled down the light, it is not
only accessible to you through the hole in your 'tin roof,' but
it also becomes accessible to anyone who is aware of the light
beyond.

"D'you mean *anyone* could steal my ideas?"

Anyone who has awareness enough to be searching for ideas
in the same place as your idea could see it, yes!

"Hey, that's not right, Fred!"

Could it not be a lesson in procrastination—use it or lose it—?

"You really *do* know me, don't you! But just a minute."
Davy's head was to one side. "All that good stuff about
bringing these ideas into consciousness, and the light
beyond—that could also work the other way, couldn't it?"

Now it's you *who's getting smart,* Fred smiled. *Yes, that's*
quite true: it would be your *consciousness that found it drifting*
on the astral. But as your awareness develops, you will come
to understand that it really doesn't matter. Your life will
become much more in tune when you can free yourself from
the need to overcome competition and the 'more' syndrome.

123

"That makes me feel better," said Davy with a smile. "Tell me some more, Fred."

You may have noticed, and many people assume it to be only a coincidence, that many of the great and major inventions seem to occur in various parts of the world simultaneously. Do you think the great modern developments and innovations that occur in the major industrial countries 'crop up' all at the same time, just like that?

"That's interesting isn't it! Now you come to think of it, things *do* seem to work like that, don't they? The more you think about it, the more you're right."

Not only in material developments but in the animal kingdom too. Research has shown that a group of monkeys on one side of the world developed and learned to do new things, while a similar group on the other side of the world began doing the same simultaneously.

"Is that a fact! Well, I would have thought that that was pretty conclusive!"

It's Group Consciousness. Do you need to have 'evidence,' Davy?

"No, but it's nice when it checks out, isn't it?" They both laughed.

GETTING TO THE FLOW

Davy loved his conversations with Fred, even though they often left him feeling intensely frustrated.

Have you ever noticed how sometimes everything in your life seems to flow naturally and easily, and sometimes it does not? Fred asked.

"Sure I have," replied Davy; "but most often it does not!" Still, Davy sensed that more of Fred's beautiful wisdom was imminent.

When things just seem to happen easily and when you least expect them . . . it's so beautiful! said Fred wistfully.

"What I have noticed, sometimes, is that when I give up on something, or stop wanting things, *that's* when they turn up."

Yes, exactly! And that is just what I want to focus on now. We call it getting to the flow.

"You mean 'flow' as in *river?*"

Exactly. Just sit and watch a river, and feel the great momentum of it all. It's awesome!

"But some rivers only flow slowly," said Davy.

They do indeed; but just try to stop them, and you will understand what I am getting at! Whether they flow gently or cascade in torrents, they are unstoppable. They have an energy that will carry anything and everything along in their path. Try wading across a river—even a very gently flowing one—and feel the great force of water against you.

"Yeah; I used to swim in the river when I was a kid. Looked so slow and peaceful, yet try to swim across . . . wow! we'd get carried way downstream."

Did you ever try to swim against the flow, Davy?

"Sure. We would *try*—but it was impossible. No matter how strong your swimming was, you'd end up going backwards. It would take every ounce of energy just to stay still."

Can you think of anything else that is like that?

"Anything else . . ." Davy's head dropped to one side again in thought.

Would you say that your whole life *has been like that?*

"Like swimming the river, you mean?"

Yes: working and struggling as hard as you possibly could just to stay where you were.

"Hey, that's magic, Fred! Yeah, that's *exactly* how my life was. In fact, most of the time I was going *backwards* where I couldn't keep up."

Fred smiled, delighted that his analogy had achieved the desired result. *I think that is a perfect example, don't you, Davy?*

"Sure; that was the story of my life: swimming against the current and not getting anywhere."

So when you were a boy swimming in the river, how would you get from one side to the other if the current was too strong to swim against?

"Oh, that was a breeze. We would run way upstream, dive in, and let the flow take us across." Davy's mouth fell open at the sudden realization. Fred articulated it:

Why do so many struggle against the currents of their lives when, if they would just walk upstream and learn about the easy way, their life would work for *them and carry them gently to where they wanted to go?*

Davy felt the flow of love in his heart. He thought, "All these things that Fred is teaching are just so simple and so obvious —yet so elusive!"

* * *

Why would he *not* think that life could be easier? Was it because people tended to be like sheep and followed the crowd, thinking if everyone else is having a tough time, that must be how it is! That must be the only way! As he thought, his whole life spun before him revealing all the examples of how he had done everything the hard way, swimming against the stream.

* * *

"If I'd only known you when I was young, Fred, life would have been so different!"

You are always young. Nothing has changed. I have always been there to guide and help you.

"So you keep saying; but I didn't know, did I?"

You didn't believe, Davy. There is a magic in believing.

"I know that *now;* but how can you believe if you don't know what to believe *in?*"

Spiritual poverty, not lack of material things, is the cause of so much human suffering.

"What does *that* mean?"

Being unaware of the existence of one's spiritual self.

"Oh, I'm learning about *you*, Fred! But I must admit that I never had a lot of time for religion."

*We are not talking about religion, Davy. Religion is the
spiritual beliefs of others; and while they may not be wrong or
incorrect, they can be just so much dogma.*

"You mean that they don't quite 'get it.' "

*Something like that, Davy. Many religious accounts have
become a little distorted, and people have become a little
disillusioned, which is all a shame, don't you think?*

"Well, I sure wish I'd known about all the things you've been
teaching me, that's for sure! I know my life would have been
a whole lot different than it was."

*But we are digressing, Davy. Let me see, what were we
talking about? Ah, yes—the flow. Have you ever noticed that
when you are in the flow and feeling good, everything seems
to happen so effortlessly?*

"Sure; everything is so easy."

Exactly; and that is what I want to focus on now.

"I remember, when I was interested in playing golf, the
harder I tried to make a perfect shot, the worse it got."

Therein lies the secret of success in any field, said Fred.

"What are you telling me, Fred? That I shouldn't try so
hard?"

129

In effect, yes—although the process is more subtle than that. When you were idly practicing your golf shots in the back yard, on your own and without any pressure . . .

"Oh, I could do nothing wrong then!" Davy interrupted excitedly. "That's magic! If only it could be like that for real!"

Well, let's try to understand why. Fred paused a moment. *What is different between playing golf in your back yard and playing on the golf course?*

"There's no one breathing down your neck all the time when you play in the yard."

Anything else?

Davy went into his thinking mode, with his head to one side. "Yeah; there's no one watching and putting you off."

Right. So if anyone watches you, it puts you off your game.

"Sure it does!"

So if anyone is watching you, it makes you try harder to make a good shot; and as a result, you actually make a bad shot—?

"I know that sounds funny, but it's exactly true."

Oh, I know it's right; it is exactly right! And it holds true for

*just about everything we do in our material lives. You see,
Davy, wealth and prosperity flow into your life when you are
unattached to them. That's what is meant when we speak of
'God manifesting through you.' You cannot force it. When you
let it go and stop trying, it will flow to you. In fact, the harder
you try, the more it will elude you.*

"I've never heard you speak a truer word, Fred. That is the
story of my whole life! But why is no one down here telling
everyone about all this good stuff, instead of watching them
all suffer as I did?"

*Because they are not ready. They would not believe, even if
they were told. Think how you were, Davy. Would you have
believed all the things you now know to be true?*

"No way, José!" he said, laughing. "I would have sent them
on their way, just as I did all those do-good Bible-punchers
that wanted to preach . . . Sorry, Fred; was that being rude
again?"

Oh no. Sadly, I can only agree with you, Davy.

"Well, they *did* make themselves a pain. And they were
always whiter-than-white goody-goody types."

So you see how difficult it is to get people to listen.

"Yes—but *you* are different, Fred. Everything you've told me
just makes so much sense!"

*They thought that what they wanted to teach you made sense;
indeed, how do you know that their information was any
different from mine?*

"Oh, you can tell . . . you've only got to look at 'em."

*It's not good to be judgmental, Davy. Until people can
separate the spiritual from the religious, there will always be
this problem. The two are very much the same yet very, very
different—another paradox!*

"Even *I* know that now; I've even learned what a paradox
is!"

They laughed together for a moment. "I know you said that
many of the rules of the material world are the opposite of the
laws of the spiritual Universe, Fred; so how could anyone
even begin to understand?"

*It's not so much a matter of understanding as it is a question
of knowing.*

"Either way, how does anyone even begin to learn what the
difference is between spiritual and religious laws if they don't
even know that there *is* a difference between them? Mention
the word *spirit* and they think you're talking about ghosts or
booze. Mention the word *God* and they label that as Religion.
Either way, they don't want to know, so you're in for trouble
for nothing! Even *you* must admit, Fred, that it's a bit
confusing!"

*If you can just begin from the point that everything in the
Universe is perfect and just accept that all is as it should be
right now, then the rest will begin to fall into place.*

"But think of all those millions of . . ."

*Just concentrate on you. You are the only person you can
affect. When you discover the truth for yourself, the 'other
shoe' will drop.*

"Mmmm, yeah; you're right."

*Just learn and understand. Light your own light, Davy, and
then not only you but many others will begin to see. You will
become a connection that will light the way for many more.
Remember that everyone is a spiritual being in a physical
body. Many haven't got to that understanding yet, but it
doesn't change the facts. The rules still apply to them,
whether or not they understand the nature of things.*

Davy looked to Fred, their communication continuing far
beyond their words.

"There are millions of people like me who would do anything
to know and understand the stuff you are teaching. It's so
interesting and directly affects their lives. These are things you
can *do* to make changes—as you told me, 'to take control.'
You really know your stuff, Fred!'' said Davy.

*Thank you, Davy. What you are really saying is that you are
beginning to believe in yourself and the ways of the Universe.*

After a moment's thought, Davy agreed. "Yeah, I guess I *am* at that!" They enjoyed a brief moment of knowing silence.

"Fred . . . could I ask you something?" said Davy, his head to one side (his thinking mode).

Of course.

"What I'd like to know is, with all your learning and stuff, what is the . . ."

I think it's time we shared that, don't you? interrupted Fred.

"How did you know what I was going to say? You're reading my mind again!"

It's so much more convenient and so much less cumbersome, don't you think? said Fred.

"Oh, I don't know; I like to hear what I've got to say!" Davy laughed.

If that's how you are comfortable, then fine. Fred paused, changing track. *I am going to tell you the greatest secret of all.* He spoke softly, answering the question that Davy was going to ask.

"How many 'greatest secrets' are there?" asked Davy.

There are many beautiful truths I have already revealed to you . . . but there is one secret that is priced higher than any other. Fred began.

"What is that?"

It is the secret from which all truth emanates.

"Okay, what is it?" Davy was becoming impatient.

Failure to understand this secret has brought some great religions to the edge of failure. It is also the one factor that all religions have in common. Fred paused and smiled at Davy's growing impatience. *It seems strange how the most basic principle of Life can so often become neglected and even distorted.*

"How can that be?"

Who knows? By self-imposed rules and dogma, maybe.

"I don't understand. Run that by me again, Fred."

When we have a truth—a secret if you like—that frees us from pain and hardship, a truth that by its very nature is so beautifully simple, it can still be very difficult for many to accept. It is as though there were a human need for any very simple or profound truth to be difficult or complex.

"I don't know . . . but you're the teacher. You haven't even told me what the secret is yet."

The most beautifully simple facts are so often made out to be complicated that their very simplicity becomes complexity. That is often how it is with the greatest of all secrets, the Secret of Secrets, if you like, said Fred.

"That sounds like pretty powerful stuff to me, Fred!"

Fred looked deeply into Davy's eyes. *It is. It truly is. The very essence of Life is right here now. The Source of all things is right here within us, in this moment, now.*

"It *is?*"

Yes—the very Source that created the whole Universe, which created everything, is here, within you, in this moment, now.

"And everyone else . . ."

Of course. It is the very essence of life.

"Whew! D'you mean . . . God?"

If that is the name you choose to give to the One Divine Creator, then yes. The moment was charged with emotion. *There is but one Creator. You may call It whatever you will— God, Buddha, Source, Spirit, He, She, or It, Jack or Jimmy— it doesn't matter in the slightest. What does matter is your understanding that there is only One and that One is within you, everyone, and everything. Isn't that beautiful, Davy?* His words charged the atmosphere with love and understanding.

"Whew!" said Davy, breaking the silence.

Don't speak for a moment, Davy. Just drink in the reality of it . . . the Secret of Secrets. That, within you, in this very moment, is the One Divine Spirit that created all things . . . What do you think of that? Fred asked quietly.

"Well," Davy began with a sharp intake of air, "I must admit I thought that the Secret of Secrets would be . . . at least like a treasure map that pointed to something. You know, Like 'X marks the spot'!"

Fred's face beamed a most beautiful smile. *Yes, that is* exactly *what it is. Isn't it exciting?*

"Hold up a minute! Is there something I'm missing here, or have you just blown a fuse?"

No; I'm just so excited!

"I can see that; but what *makes* you so excited? Lay it on me again; I must have missed it the first time." Davy's mind was racing.

It is the Secret of Secrets—the most important truth you can understand, Fred began again.

Davy took another deep breath, ready to verbalize his frustrations, when Fred held a finger to his lips for silence.

The key to everything you have ever dreamed about is within you. That great Source of all things, the Giver of all life, all wisdom, all prosperity, lies within *you, Davy—within everyone.*

"That's the secret?"

Yes: the Source of all is within. *Isn't that wonderful?*

"What d'you mean—within me?"

It is the very essence *of who you are, the very Life Force within you. So often, when you have been having a tough time, I have heard you say, 'There must be more to life than this!'*

"Yeah, that's true; I have. I've always thought that there must be more to life than what I was getting," Davy thought aloud.

Is this not a beautiful answer to that? Think about it like this, Davy: the Source that manifests all things is within *you. So don't you find it exciting that the same Source could create* anything *through* you?

"I would find it exciting if some of Its good stuff were to come my way!"

Oh but it does, Davy! said Fred. *You must understand that everyone has the gift of free will—to be able to think your own thoughts. We have already talked about that. 'Ask and it will be given unto you.'*

"Yeah, I've heard that before."

If you can believe that the Source of all things is within you—ask for those things you desire. Then it will be done unto you as you desire.

"You're kidding!" Davy fairly exclaimed.

Everything that you had, everything that happened to you, was all created in the same way, said Fred.

"That's nothing to shout about; it's all been a disaster!"

Exactly; and that is the perfect reflection of what your thoughts were. 'As you believe, so it will be done unto you'!

"You're getting religious on me!"

No. I am reflecting the truth. Take a moment to reflect on various high and low points of your life and you will discover for yourself that they were a perfect manifestation of what you were thinking, or your attitude, back then.

Davy thought for a moment, then threw his arms in the air in despair. "Yeah, I can see it now. It all makes perfect sense now that you've explained things to me. But how was I to know back then?"

How did you learn anything, *Davy?*

"Search me, Fred! By doing it, I guess."

Exactly. How does a baby learn not to touch a fire?

"By touching it a couple of times and getting burned, right?"

Right. You've got it, Davy.

"That's the story of my life—only I got burned *every* time!"

It does not have to be like that. All this knowledge is within us because the Source and Creator of all things is within us. This wisdom is already within, if we will only learn to listen. Because much of our teaching is from peers, we accept that all learning is a process of trial and error.

"I can surely relate to that, Fred."

But it doesn't have to be like that. The sooner we can trust the Inner Source, the quicker we learn the easy way—that is, instinctively to know *that the fire will burn and cause pain. Then there's no need to touch it and learn the hard way.*

"Does that apply to everything?"

Of course. It is a universal law, and it all stems from the understanding that the Source of all things is within and not without. It is not separate from us. We are one! It is all within

us, Davy! Understand: 'the Kingdom of Heaven is within.'
You don't have to search for it 'out there.' You already have
it, in here. Fred touched his heart.

"Whew, Fred!" said Davy after a moment. "It all makes so
much sense when you know . . ."

That is the most important secret I can give you. Take it now
and use it and your life will never be the same again.

"What d'you mean?" Davy asked, looking around him. "I
thought it was all over, now that I'm . . ."

You still have many tasks to fulfill in this life. It's not over yet,
Fred said quietly.

"What d'you mean, 'in this life'? I've finished with that life!
That's why I'm here . . . isn't it?"

No, Davy; it is not your time yet. Fred spoke with sadness.

"What d'you mean, *not my time?* I'm already here, aren't I?"
There was no reply. Instead, Fred directed his gaze back
towards the frantic earthly group struggling over Davy's body.
Davy began to panic.

"What's happening?? Fred, *help me! . . . What's*
happening?"

You are going back, Davy, Fred spoke gently.

"No! I don't want to go back! I'm happy here . . . I don't . . ."

But you asked to . . .

"No; I didn't mean it . . . I want to stay with you!" Davy was panicking.

You must, *Davy! It is not time yet. There is still much work for you to do.*

"No, Fred! I still don't know anything . . . what to do . . ."

Yes you do. You have learned much here.

"Will I remember it all when I get back?"

Your searching will be easier now, Fred replied mystically.

"I won't remember, will I! You didn't give me a direct answer. I'll *still* not know your secrets! You're *still* not telling me! Oh, Fred!" Davy pleaded. "It's going to be like a beautiful dream: when I wake up, I won't remember anything —only that I've had a dream! I don't *want* to go back! That life is over for me! I don't want it any more!"

Davy's words were pleading and coming faster as time began to return.

"I must have been a real 'bozo' down there. I don't want to

be like that any more! How will I ever understand all this stuff
on my own? . . . I never read any books . . . never been any
good when it comes to learning. I've never been so happy as I
am . . .''

You will be as happy, Davy. Tears appeared on Fred's face.
*Life will never be the same again. You will need to be
strong . . . to adapt. It's a time of great change.*

"But I still don't know what to do!''

You will. Just follow your knowing. *Remember, we are always
there. You are never alone. Keep some time to be quiet and go
within. We will be waiting.*

"Meditate, yes—you mean I should meditate and do
treatments. But I don't know if I can. I've never done it.''

You can learn. There are many changes awaiting you, Davy.

"What d'you mean?''

*It will be a period of rapid growth. Excitement. You will
become a wonderful teacher.*

"Teacher! Oh! Now I'm sure you've flipped! Can't you
remember I got two out of eighty on my last school report?
And that was for spelling my name right!''

*Always remember, you are a beautiful person, a vital link.
You are so important . . .*

"I can't hear you, Fred!" Davy screamed as Fred's voice faded. "Something's happening . . . *Fred!*"

Just remember: we are inseparable . . . always together . . .

"Fred! I'm going! . . . I'm . . . going . . . I'm feeling cold . . ." Davy tried to say, "I love you," but the words wouldn't come.

Remember, Davy, Fred called after him. *Love and happiness . . . love and happiness . . . that is all there is . . .* His words echoed into the distance, then were gone.

TRANSITION

The EKG monitors and ventilators were keeping Davy's material body working. Tubes and wires monitored all the bodily functions, while blinking lights and traces of jagged neon lines each revealed their part of the story. Eyes exchanged glances as they peered up from the work in hand.

* * *

"CVP reading?" called a voice watching the drip.

"We've got a trace . . . " called another green-gowned figure.

"Keep going," replied another anxious voice.

* * *

The gowned figures were succeeding in their struggle. Davy began to feel again the restrictions of a body about him. Again his body ricocheted as the shock paddles discharged their electrical jolt, sending his body into an involuntary spasm. The voices grew more excited as the tide turned on their long efforts to save his life.

* * *

"Keep going. I think . . . we've got him," spoke one of the gowned figures as the activity continued with renewed fervor.

"More fluid," murmured another.

"Good; blood pressure back to 80 . . . increasing."

"Keep a finger on that pulse," said another.

* * *

Davy was a person again. Consciousness had returned to his body. He could feel the touch of hands on his body, but there was no pain. Sounds and muffled voices came into his mind. There were lights—bright lights and colors, white and green. He became aware of a figure huddled over him blurred and out of focus. Fingers roughly pried open an eyelid and shone a light close to his eye. He could feel someone's breath close to his face. "Slight reaction . . ." the voice said, repeating the procedure with the other eye, and concluding, "Equal response."

* * *

"Pulse is getting stronger . . . steadying . . ." came another voice from within the jabbering.

* * *

Davy made a groan that was a signal of much delight and renewed
activity. He slowly began to feel his body again. His life was
flowing back. The medical staff, which had been toiling to save
his physical life, had won its victory. He was functioning within
his body again.

Although his thoughts were muddled, he was now aware of what
was going on. The lingering experience with Fred was now fading
fast from his mind, like a beautiful dream. Davy wanted it to go
on forever, but he was powerless to stop it from disappearing like
a wave merging with the beach. He was left with only the after-
glow of knowing that something wonderful had happened, yet he
was unable to remember exactly what.

With great physical effort Davy moved his fingers, eliciting yet
greater excitement from his attendants.

* * *

"Blood pressure 100 . . . steadying."

* * *

Davy was clearly aware of being attached to this cumbersome
body, reluctantly accepting that he was back, a physical person
again. What was it Fred had told him? "A spiritual being having
a physical experience . . . or resuming one": he remembered
that. So badly did he want to retain all the wonderful teachings
and revelations that had been so lovingly revealed to him.

Yet, however much he tried, he could only remember the warm
and comforting *knowing* that there is so much more to life than
appears on this material plane.

Davy knew that his material life had started again and he knew
that it was going to be different this time.